F

MW01120244

Can Themba (formally D'Orsay Canadoce Themba) was born in June 1924, one of a family of four, in Pretoria's Marabastad location. After schooling there and in Pietersburg, he was the first candidate to win a Mendi memorial scholarship to Fort Hare University College in the Eastern Cape where he completed his BA in 1947. That year he published his first short story in *The Fort Harian*. At Rhodes University he completed his teacher's diploma. *Zonk*, the picture magazine, carried his early poems.

He began his career as a teacher at Western Native Township High School, and also at the Central Indian High School in Fordsburg, placing his first commercial short story in *Drum* in 1953. When a month later, as a bachelor of twenty-eight, he won the first *Drum* short story competition with his 'Mob Passion', he joined the magazine's staff. By 1954 he was launching as its editor the magazine *Africa!*, billed as *Drum*'s younger sister. He also steered a column called 'Us: Can Says' for *Drum*'s newer sister, the Sunday tabloid, *The Golden City Post*, and became *Drum*'s assistant editor. He contributed notably to *Africa South* and *The New African* as well. He was instrumental in founding Nat Nakasa's *The Classic* literary magazine, with his 'The Suit' as the leading item in the first issue.

Fired from *Drum* for bingeing, Can von Themba, as he styled himself, went into voluntary exile in Swaziland, from where from 1962 he contributed columns to the rival newspaper *Elethu*, and where his wife Anne of 1959 and the first of their two baby daughters duly joined him. In 1966 he became a banned person, no longer to be quoted in South Africa. (This prohibition was not lifted till 1982.) Employed as an English teacher once again, at St Joseph's Catholic Mission School near Manzini, while reading a newspaper in bed he died of a coronary thrombosis in September 1967.

Two posthumous collections of Themba's work have concentrated on his prolific journalism and other pieces published mostly under the *Drum* banner. By contrast, this selection specialises in his creative work, particularly for other outlets, written over a twelve-year period, and includes many previously unavailable pieces. When the Congress of South African Writers opened its library in Fordsburg in 1989, it was named in memory of Can Themba.

'Can Themba's own story about Johannesburg in this collection has an intensity and closeness to his scene which are more powerful than any white writing could be. There is no longer any need to tell Africans they are not chickens but eagles.'
The Times Literary Supplement *on* Darkness and Light, *March 1959*

'As vignettes of life in the African locations round Johannesburg in the 1950s, Can Themba's short stories are of lasting interest.'
Richard Rive (1973)

'The rebel par excellence.'
Es'kia Mphahlele in 1985

'Themba helped to record and create the voices, images and values of the black urban culture of the 1950s which, in the aftermath of war-time industrial expansion, was struggling to assert its permanence and identity.'
Michael Chapman in a 1988 paper

'How can we forget that Can Themba's knowledge of English, his passing the subject with a distinction, was legendary in his day? As school-boys we got to know about the writer Can Themba who was a "walking dictionary".'
Njabulo Ndebele in Current Writing *(1989)*

'The most fluent user of English in the Africa of his time.'
Taban Lo Liyong in a paper delivered in 1999

REQUIEM FOR SOPHIATOWN

Can Themba

PENGUIN BOOKS

Published by Penguin Random House South Africa (Pty) Ltd
Company Reg No 1953/000441/07
The Estuaries No 4, Oxbow Crescent, Century Avenue, Century City, 7441,
South Africa
PO Box 1144, Cape Town, 8000, South Africa
www.penguinrandomhouse.co.za

ISBN-13: 978-0-143-18548-2
ISBN-10: 0-143-18548-9

Typeset by DKS Design in 10 on 12.5 pt Palatino
Cover design: African Icons
Printed and bound by Novus Print, a Novus Holdings company

Penguin Random House is committed to a sustainable future for our business,
our readers and our planet. This book is made from Forest Stewardship
Council® certified paper.

Contents

Notes on Sources

The first collection of Can Themba's writings was *The Will to Die*, edited by Donald Stuart and Roy Holland for the Heinemann African Writers Series in London in 1972. Once his work became unbanned in South Africa, David Philip in Cape Town issued a local edition in 1982 in his Africasouth series. This was followed by *The World of Can Themba*, a further selection of his pieces, edited by Essop Patel for Johannesburg's Ravan Press in 1985.

All the items included here, however, are freshly edited from original sources, and reproduced in their original order, as follows:

'Passionate Stranger'
Themba's first substantial short story, written in the melodramatic popular vein appropriate to tabloids, as are the next four stories. Carried in the monthly *Drum* magazine under the editorship of Anthony Sampson. He described Themba as 'a slender, bony man with a sensitive face, and a misleadingly innocent expression' who jived like a 'clockwork duck'. The *Drum* author box number 6 described D'Orsay Can Themba as a teacher with 'writing as one of his chief interests'. Published in the edition of March 1953 and in the international edition a month later.

'Mob Passion'
Published in the South African *Drum* in May 1953 as the winning entry of their Great International Short Story Contest, for which 'stories in English and every African language have poured into the *Drum* office from Lagos to Cape Town, from Bermuda to London. Long ones and short ones, good ones and bad ones and by the closing date there was a pile of over one thousand stories to read.' One of the judges, Peter Abrahams – recently in the *Drum* offices on a return visit to Johannesburg

after fourteen years abroad – commended Themba's 'unusual literary promise', while awarding second prize to Nigeria's Cyprian Ekwensi and third to another home-boy, William 'Bloke' Modisane.

Nxumalo (right) hands Themba his prize
(Copyright Jurgen Schadeberg, 1952)

Henry Nxumalo tracked Themba down to his address to award him his £50 cheque. He recorded:

At the top of a noisy street in Sophiatown, sitting reading on the stoep of his house, we found *Drum's* winning author. He took us to his tiny bed-sitting room. Books of poetry, short stories, reference books and half-typed over sheets of paper were piled high on a table at the end of his bed.

'I must wait till they're all asleep,' Themba remarked patiently. 'I don't start writing till after twelve sometimes. If I'm to get anything done, I must work until three and often four in the morning. But it's tiring on the eyes, working by lamplight.

'I also walk up and down the streets for hours, forming stories in the back of my mind. Then when I come to write them down, they are in one piece ready to be written. But don't think I'm a believer in writing by inspiration only – no, it's just plain hard work all the way. As for hobbies, I have none other than my reading and writing.'

In the August 1953 *Drum* Nxumalo wrote of his newfound friend in his 'Talk o' the Rand' column:

Drum's own story contest winner, Can Themba – his last name means 'trust' – is a romance yarn merchant in double trouble. It all starts when Johannesburg's Western High School students who know him better as their English teacher admire him both as a teacher and a love expert, but fight shy of asking him direct questions about these things. They write to *Drum* about him and he is embarrassed.

'Perhaps they take my name literally,' says our author, whose fanmail comes from as far afield as Nigeria. 'After all, I am an ignorant bachelor. The problems they send me only help to swell my ideas for future passionate stories – and moola!'

'Mob Passion' was chosen by Peggy Rutherfoord for inclusion in her *Darkness and Light* anthology, prefaced by this note:

> A story told against a background of the 1951-1952 riots in Newclare, a township eight miles west of Johannesburg. Fighting broke out between a gang, composed largely of Basutos working on the Rand mines, who called themselves 'Russians', and the Civil Guards. The Russians had been terrorising the people of that district, and the Civil Guards were formed of members of other tribes, in order to protect themselves and the people of the township. It was after the Civil Guards had taken the law into their own hands and made reprisals on their enemy that the strife turned into gang warfare.

'The Nice Time Girl'
Published in the local *Drum* of May 1954, and in the West African edition of July. By now Es'kia Mphahlele (then known as Ezekiel or 'Zeke') was his fiction editor. As his fellow contributor, Bloke Modisane, wrote: 'The short story is used by us as a short cut to get some things off one's chest in quick time. The situation is so vast and the best way to communicate is to pinpoint the incidents.'

When another staff member, Arthur Maimane, contributed a short story to Volume 1, Number 1 of Themba's *Africa!* in March 1954, as an in-joke he described his classmate of old as 'usually the most cheerful boy in the men's hostel. But now he was a brooding fly-by-night, reading Shakespeare's *Othello* and quoting verses from the Moor's jealous, heartbroken rantings!' *Africa!* also included the American Langston Hughes as a regular columnist.

'Forbidden Love'
First published in *Drum*, November 1955.

'Marta'
Billed as 'D. Can Themba's first story of life in the racy shebeens of Sophiatown.' Carried in *Drum*, July 1956, by which date Sylvester Stein was beginning his two-year stint as *Drum's* editor, with Themba as his assistant editor.

'Henry Nxumalo'
The murder of Mr Drum over Christmas 1956 occasioned this Themba memorial article, placed prominently in *Drum* in the following February. The middle section beginning 'When I started the column ...', however, is inserted from *The Golden City Post* of a fortnight before (on 13 January 1957). By November 1958, *Post* was able to feature a story that one of Nxumalo's suspected killers had been reprieved for lack of evidence, while the three other suspects – apparently paid £105 for assassinating him – were still on the loose.

'Preface'
Written in the *Drum* offices for *Darkness and Light: An Anthology of African Writing*, edited by Peggy Rutherfoord and published eventually in London by Faith Press in 1958 for Drum Publications of Johannesburg. This turned out to be a landmark collection heralding the rise of postwar writing continent wide, inspired by the coming independence of the Gold Coast in 1957.

'Here it is at Last'
Review of *Darkness and Light*, as it became available in South Africa, in the May *Drum* of 1959 (published in East Africa in June).

'Spot Letter'
A hoax item in *Drum* of December 1960, for which a certain 'C T' of Johannesburg was one guinea richer. After an interregnum during which Can Themba, the photographer Jurgen Schadeberg and copy-editor Humphrey Tyler appear to

have run *Drum*, Tom Hopkinson took over as editor, soon to terminate Themba's contract. Only two further items in this collection derive from the *Drum* network; from here his style matures accordingly.

'Requiem for Sophiatown'
Included in the quarterly review *Africa South*, edited by Ronald Segal in Cape Town, in Volume 3, Number 3, of April-June 1959. When Langston Hughes edited the follow-up to *Darkness and Light* – his *An African Treasury* of 1960 – he included this essay as a payback. He also remarked on how Themba's colleagues and other contributors of his, like Mphahlele, Modisane, Maimane and Todd Matshikiza, had by then gone into exile from South Africa.

'The Bottom of the Bottle'
Themba's second piece for Segal, who by then had left South Africa as well, publishing his review as *Africa South in Exile*. Featured in Volume 5, Number 3, of April-June 1961.

'Crepuscule', 'Kwashiorkor', 'The Will to Die' and 'Ten to Ten'
First published posthumously in *The Will to Die*, with the last two subsequently carried over into *The World of Can Themba*. From typescripts supplied by Themba's widow.

'The Urchin'
Finalised and submitted to Mphahlele from Manzini in Swaziland as one of eight prizewinning stories in a contest which had been open to writers of all races, organised by the South African Centre of the International PEN Club, another finalist being Casey Motsisi. As a tribute to his former staffman, the new *Drum* editor Cecil Eprile launched it in April 1963. The volume edited by Mphahlele, *African Writing Today*, in which 'The Urchin' was at last included, was published by Penguin in 1967.

'The Suit'
Also in 1963, shortly before his departure from Johannesburg, Themba produced this chestnut, perhaps the most reproduced piece of fiction of his generation. Since Jim Bailey, the *Drum* proprietor, had suspended the magazine's fiction section in 1957, as Themba notes, plans had been afoot to launch an alternative, black-controlled outlet for creative efforts. Volume 1, Number 1 of *The Classic*, edited by Nathaniel Nakasa, was duly launched from a postal address in Johannesburg that year, with 'The Suit' as its leading item. Also included was a poem of Themba's called 'Dear God', which begins:

God, you gave me colour,
Rich, sun-drenched, chocolate,
And you gave me valour,
Enough for Love, for Hate ...

Among a stellar cast were other future names such as Lewis Nkosi and Richard Rive. By the time Nadine Gordimer and Lionel Abrahams reproduced 'The Suit' in their *South African Writing Today*, also published by Penguin in 1967, its inclusion was one reason for the automatic proscription of that anthology.

Once Themba's work was allowed legally to reappear in *The Will to Die*, and subsequently in *The World of Can Themba*, 'The Suit' took on a life of its own: in 1993 Peter Esterhuysen made a *Deep Cuts* graphic adaptation of it and in 1994 Chris van Wyk reworked it for Viva Books for younger readers; in 1993 Mothobi Mutloatse adapted it as a stage play for the Duze Ensemble and it was further workshopped by Barney Simon for a Market Theatre production, eventually taken over by Peter Brook in Paris; a subsequent stage version was made by Christopher Weare in 2002. For the Fantastic Flying Fish Dance Company Boyzie Cekwana choreographed 'The Suit' as a dance drama, which premiered at the Grahamstown National Arts Festival in 2002. Discussions for filming are in progress. The NELM database lists no fewer than fifteen further anthologisations (translations excluded).

'Quoth He'
Written for *The Classic*, with a note scrawled in ink: 'Nat, Just call it "Quoth He" ' (although the typescript is headed 'Quoth God'). Either because of Nakasa's hasty departure after the third number of *The Classic* in 1964, or owing to Themba's then undetermined status over the border, this piece never saw print. Found amongst the collection of *Classic* material deposited by Nakasa's successor, Barney Simon, in the National English Literary Museum, Grahamstown. To the museum's curators due acknowledgements should be made for this item, appearing here for the first time, as well as for access to their extensive holdings of Themba material.

'Through Shakespeare's Africa'
An essay submitted from Swaziland to the founder-editor, Randolph Vigne in Cape Town, of the radical monthly *The New African*, which carried it in Volume 2, Number 8 on 21 September 1963.

'The Fugitives'
As for the above item from *The New African*, this one has never previously been collected. A sketch included by Vigne in Volume 3, Number 3 on 28 March 1964, shortly before *The New African* also moved to London, where Lewis Nkosi became its literary editor.

'The Dube Train'
Submitted to Mphahlele who, together with his co-editor Ellis Ayitey Komey, included it in their frequently reprinted *Modern African Stories*, the anthology first published by Faber and Faber in London in 1964. Their blurb liked to quote the review of *The Times* of London, which singled out Themba's 'short, harsh sketch of petty violence on a Monday morning

train'. The following year Gerald Moore in *Transition*, recently founded as a literary journal in Kampala, while registering his distress at Themba's non-person rank in his homeland, remarked of this item:

> His prose gives the story its cool effectiveness. The event, dramatic enough in itself, also serves to gather for us all the desperate energy of a life in which every man or woman rushes forward, crushing whatever falls in their path, in their haste to reach a goal which savagely rejects them.

In fact, this piece was a reworking of an article of Themba's called 'Terror in the Trains', included in *Drum* in October 1957.

'The Boy with the Tennis-Racket'
Drum used this tribute to Nakasa, posted in by the exiled sage as requested, on 15 August 1965 – by which date the colourful monthly had been reduced to being a weekly pull-out supplement to *The Golden City Post* each Sunday. This was positively Themba's last appearance in South Africa, as by the time in 1966 *The Classic* attempted to reprint this memoir of their founder, in Volume 2, Number 1, Themba had become a banned person, no longer to be quoted. Notoriously the offending pages had to be scissored out of each issue. In turn, *The Classic* of Volume 2, Number 4 of 1968 devoted major space to tributes to the late Can Themba (by Casey Motsisi, Harry Mashabela, Stan Motjuwadi and Juby Mayet).

'Cayenne Pepper', 'Through Can's Lens' and 'The Last Shebeen'
Unrecorded in all the existing reference works and other retrieval systems is the detail that, once Themba was settled in Swaziland Protectorate, he took steady employment with another newspaper group, financed by the South African Bantu Industrial Corporation Ltd, as opposition to the *Drum* stable. To their weekly *Elethu* (subsequently *Elethu Mirror* and

Our Own Mirror), from Volume 1, Number 14 of 4 August 1962, Can Themba contributed an occasional column called 'Cayenne Pepper ... through Can's Lens'. The three excerpts here, dating from 11 August, 15 September and 29 September, never having been collected before, represent his next to last words to see print in South Africa in his lifetime.

Themba at work in Sophiatown
(Copyright Jurgen Schadeberg, 1952)

Passionate Stranger

Osbourne Ledwaba was bitter against his father for the way the old man had treated his friend, Reginald Tshayi, with whom he had come to Chebeng to spend a short vacation. Why did he call him a Joburg tsotsi? Surely, it was rude!

He stole a glance at Reggie who seemed unaffected by his father's rudeness.

'Reg,' began Osbourne, 'I'm sorry.'

'Nonsense, Ossie,' Reggie replied, 'fathers are like that the world over.'

As he spoke, in came the most beautiful creature with a tray of tea things. She put them down on the little table before saying hello in the loveliest voice and with the sweetest smile.

Osbourne introduced her with obvious pride. 'This is Ellen, Reg. The prettiest sister anybody ever had. Kid, this is Reg. He teaches in a high school.'

'Glad to meet you. Your brother calls me a rag, but I've a real surname, too. I'm Reginald Tshayi.'

'I hope you'll have a happy time with us. Please excuse me.' She floated out of the room.

Osbourne's father came in later and told Osbourne that they should go to the Chief's kraal to pay their respects. 'Your friend needn't bother,' concluded the old man.

'But ... but ...' Osbourne complained.

'Don't worry, Osbourne,' Reginald came to the rescue. 'This gives me a first class chance to finish off that last chapter of *Salome*.'

Osbourne left with his father. Reggie had hardly read a few lines when there came a light tap on the door. It was Ellen.

'Oh, reading?' She arched her brows so prettily. 'I saw

Osbourne and father leave, so I thought I might invite you to join me in the sitting room, if you'd like to.'

Reggie went with her. They talked about many things, but inevitably he told her of Joburg.

He did not try to thrill her, but the sincerity and fervour of his dissatisfactions spoke so vehemently that she remarked: 'You needed this holiday badly, Reggie. You know, you've a tremendous capacity for powerful emotion.' Then precipitately: 'Tell me, have you ever been in love?'

Reggie rose from his chair and sat down on the floor in front of her. He looked up into her face before he replied.

'Ellen, I *am* in love. I needed to escape the smoke and filth, the misery and degradation of Joburg to discover that something fresh and sweet is still possible in womanhood. If my declaration sounds premature and impetuous to you, forgive me. Love is on the wing and, whether I will it or no, I must join its flight. Whether I will it or no, I must love you. Destiny itself has guided my wanderings to this far place that I may lay my troubles in your bosom. Have I ever loved, you ask. How shall I say? There have been those who scratched on the surface of my life, but my soul has been virgin. Never before has my soul echoed the resounding depths or soared the giddy heights as now. What those wretched women in Joburg with their earthly desires inspired in me was retreat from the name of love. Now I know what true love can mean. Nevermore can the stars whirl and wheel the same, if you do not love me, too, Ellen. No more would the moons shed soft silver on the earth, no more would the flowers gladden the heart, the birds untune the sky. Oh nevermore! I reach for your lips, knowing I reach for the sun!'

'Too soon, Reggie. It's too soon to be true!' Ellen grasped him by the shoulder, pleading her fear.

'Two lives preordained for each other, love treads on the paths of lightning. Whether we will or no, we must discover and fulfil each other.'

'Whether we will it or no,' Ellen whispered as she sank

down on his imploring lips.

They lay in each other's arms long and still, silently contemplating this thing the gods had done. The first storm of passion spent, a great peace descended on them as soul met soul in perfect unity and their bodies intertwined like a woven whip. Deep meaning suffused their union, so that perfect understanding was achieved. And they were one.

'Reggie! Reggie!'

'Mm.' He squirmed gently in the tangle of her embrace, then lay still again.

'Reggie. Reggie, darling, father and Osbourne will soon return. We must separate ... and, Reggie, we must keep our love a secret,' she admonished. 'Father won't understand.'

'Tonight, after supper, under the big tree opposite the cattle kraal. I'll be waiting for you.' All the eagerness of his new love was in his voice.

'I'll be there, darling,' she whispered.

He went to his room, whilst she tried to tidy up the sitting room.

When Osbourne and his father returned, they were arguing heatedly. Osbourne had discovered that his father was negotiating a marriage between Ellen and Dikgang and he was filled with anger. Reggie had to intervene. He took Osbourne off and had a long talk with him.

At supper Osbourne apologised to his father. He simply said, 'Father, I'm sorry.' The meal broke up in a tense atmosphere. Reggie and Osbourne went to their room.

'Drown yourself in your trumpet, Ossie,' Reggie said to him. 'I want to take a solitary walk and sort my ideas.'

Reggie slipped out into the night and casually strolled to the big tree near the cattle kraal. He did not wait long before Ellen came. He took her in his arms and they spiralled away into a heaven where their rebel emotions could harmonise. But earth is never far from heaven, for just then Ellen's father came upon them.

'Ha!' he started. 'Who are you? Ellen! What are – So it's the Joburg tsotsi already demonstrating Joburg behaviour. You come into my house, enjoy my hospitality, bewitch my son and now you seek to seduce my daughter! Tomorrow you leave my house and never let your shadow darken its threshold again.'

'If you say so, my father,' Ellen said, 'tomorrow I leave your house with him.' The sharp menace in her voice startled her father. 'It's useless trying to tell you I love him. You wouldn't understand.'

'But what about Dikgang?'

'Go marry him yourself.'

'Get to your room! As for you, you … you …' The old man struck Reggie and spat, but Reggie did not move a hair.

Then the old man swung round in impotent rage, caught Ellen by the arm and dragged her to the house with a thousand damns.

Back in the room as Reggie was packing and Osbourne was looking glumly on, the old man reappeared. He looked wretched.

'Osbourne, I want you to come and talk sense into your sister. She's packing her clothes.'

'My father,' Osbourne interrupted quietly, almost meekly, 'when I said this evening that I'm sorry, I meant *I* at least had realised that Ellen's love affairs are not my business. And, father, I'm going to pack too.'

In his despair the old man turned to Reggie. 'You can make them stay. I beg you to dissuade them from their cruelty to their mother, and then go quietly.'

Suddenly Reggie felt very tired. The note of pain in the old man's voice sounded genuine, but his interpretation of the situation was unfair and the implications of his demand terrible. Reggie was trapped. Yet he was to be given no chance to decide. Voices were heard outside and the old man went out.

4

When he returned he was in a different mood. He was light-hearted and gay, with a malicious gleam in his eye and a smirk of cruel joy on his lips.

'Osbourne,' he said, 'there'll be a meeting in the sitting room. I want you to be present, too.'

'When, father?'

'Now.'

When Osbourne and Reggie came to the sitting room they found members of the Chief's council come to settle the question of Dikgang's bride price for Ellen.

After the introductions a grey-headed old man spoke: 'Well, Ledwaba, last time we discussed this union you virtually promised us your daughter if the bride price is right. We're instructed by the Chief not to wrangle over the number of cattle. You may, therefore, consider it settled at any number you care to fix.'

'That speeds our discussion. Shall we say twenty-five?' Old Ledwaba was happy with the turn of events. He rubbed his hands affably.

'Father,' broke in Osbourne unexpectedly. 'May I say something?'

His father frowned and shifted uneasily. But before he could say anything, the grey-headed old man said: 'Certainly, certainly.'

'I think we should display our wares before these gentlemen commit themselves to a purchase. I'm sure they'd like to see the girl.' He said it so simply that the councillors were impressed with his figure of speech. Only his father and his friend knew its stinging lash.

'A sensible suggestion,' someone muttered and old Ledwaba's protests choked in his throat. He sullenly nodded assent and Osbourne went to fetch Ellen.

After a while she appeared in the doorway.

Her father tried his last trick. 'There's no need to say anything, my child. These gentlemen merely wish to see you.'

'But I do have something to say, father. Something drastic.'

Her father sank slowly into a chair.

She turned to the men. 'My fathers, I know the woman should be silent and suffer her betters and elders to determine her fate. Still, believe me, this way is the best. You are here to make me a wife to Dikgang. What I think of him is entirely irrelevant. But you must know that I already belong to another, not so much from the wilfulness of my rebel heart, but because by the law of man and of God. I cannot go to any man as a virgin, but to the man I love.'

And she walked out.

There was uproar. Reggie gaped. Osbourne tittered.

Old Ledwaba sat bowed and broken. He hardly heard the grey-headed old man begin to speak.

'My brothers,' he said, 'let us not chatter like apes. Let us rather retire to deliberate on how to convince the Chief that we do not encourage this marriage and how to avert a crisis in the tribe. Ledwaba, we shall try to suppress the insult to the Royal House. We say no more, for we know how you suffer. Do you hear?'

He did not hear; he would not hear or tell anything any more.

Mob Passion

There was a thick crowd on Platform Two, rushing for the All Stations Randfontein train. Men, women and children were pushing madly to board the train. They were heaving and pressing, elbows in faces, bundles bursting, weak ones kneaded. Even at the opposite side people were balancing precariously to escape being shoved off the platform. Here and there deft fingers were exploring unwary pockets. Somewhere an outraged dignity was shrieking stridently, vilely cursing someone's parentage. Fuller and fuller the carriages became. With a jerk the electric train moved out of the station.

'Whew!' panted Linga Sakwe. He gathered his few parcels upon his lap, pressing his elbows to his side pockets. He did not really have any valuables in these pockets; only long habit was working instinctively now.

Linga was a tall, slender fellow, more man than boy. He was not particularly handsome, but he had those tense eyes of the young student who was ever inwardly protesting against some wrong or other. In fact, at the moment he was not a student at all. He was working for a firm of lawyers in Market Street. He hoped to save enough money in a year or two to return to university to complete an arts degree which he had been forced by circumstances to abandon.

People were still heaving about in the train, but Linga was not annoyed. He knew that by Langlaagte, or perhaps Westbury, most of these folk would be gone and he would be able to breathe again. At Braamfontein many people alighted, but he was not thinking of his discomfort any more. He was thinking of Mapula now. She had promised that she would be in time for this train. That depended, of course, on whether she succeeded to persuade the staff nurse in charge of the ward in which she worked to let her off a few minutes before time.

The train slowed down. Industria. Linga anxiously looked outside. Sure enough, there she was! He gave a wolf whistle, as if he was admiring some girl he did not know. She hurried to his carriage, stepped in and sat beside him. They did not seem to know each other from Adam. An old man nearby was giving a lively narration in the grimmest terms of the murders committed at Newclare.

At Westbury the atmosphere was tense. Everybody crowded at the windows to see. Everywhere there were white policemen, heavily armed. The situation was 'under control', but everyone knew that in the soul of almost every being in this area raved a seething madness, wild and passionate, with the causes lying deep. No cursory measures can remedy, no superficial explanation can illuminate. These jovial faces that can change into masks of bloodlust and destruction with no warning on smallest provocation! There is a vicious technique faithfully applied in these riots. Each morning these people quietly rise and with a businesslike manner hurry to their work. Each evening they return to a Devil's Party, uncontrollably drawn into hideous orgies. Sometimes the violence would subside for weeks or months, and then suddenly would flare up at some unexpected spot, on some unexpected pretext.

At Newclare, too, from the train all seemed quiet. But Linga and Mapula knew the deceptive quiet meant the same even here. The train skimmed on, emptier. Only when they had passed Maraisburg did those two venture to speak to each other. Linga was Xhosa and Mapula Sotho. A Letebele and a Russian! They had to be very careful. Love in its mysterious, often ill-starred ways had flung them together.

Linga spoke first.

'Sure you saw no one who might know you?' he asked softly.

'Eh – eh,' she replied.

She fidgeted uneasily with the strap of her handbag. His hand went out and closed over her fingers. They turned simultaneously to look at each other.

A sympathetic understanding came into Linga's eyes. He smiled.

'Rather tense, isn't it?' he said.

She looked past him through the window.

'Witpoortjie!' she exclaimed. 'Come, let's go.'

They rose and went to the door. The train stopped and they went out. Together they walked to a bridge, went over the line and out by a little gate. For some two hundred yards they walked over flat stubbly ground. Then they went down a mountain cleft at the bottom of which ran a streamlet. They found a shady spot and sat down on the green grass. Then suddenly they fled into each other's arms like frightened children. The time-old ritual, ancient almost as the hills, always novel as the ever-changing skies; long they clung to each other, long and silent. Only the little stream gurgled its nonsense; these two daring hearts were lost in each other. The world, too – good, bad or indifferent – was forgotten in the glorious flux of their souls meeting and mingling.

At last Mapula spoke – half cried: 'Oh Linga! I'm afraid.'

'Here where the world is quiet?' he quoted, with infinite softness. 'No, dear, nothing can reach and harm us here.' Then with a sigh: 'Still, the cruellest thing they do is to drive two young people like guilty things to sneak off only to see each other. What is wrong with our people, Mapula?'

She did not answer. He lay musing for a long time. She could see that he was slowly getting angry. Sometimes she wished she could understand the strange indignations of his spirit and the great arguments by which he explained life. Most times she only yearned for his love.

'They do not see! They do not see!' he continued vehemently. 'They butcher one another, and they seem to like it. Where there should be brotherhood and love, there are bitter animosities. Where there should be cooperation in common adversity, there are barriers of hostility, steeling a brother's heart against a brother's misery. Sometimes, 'Pule, I understand it. We have

9

had so many dishonest leaders, and we have so often had our true leaders left in the lurch by weak-kneed colleagues and lukewarm followers that no one wishes to stick his neck out too far. Where is the courage to weld these suicidal factions into a nation? The trouble is, very few of us have a vision comprehensive enough of our destiny! I believe God has a few of us to whom He whispers in the ear! Our true history is before us, for we yet have to build, to create, to achieve. Our very oppression is the flower of opportunity. If not for History's Grand Finale, why, then, does God hold us back? Hell! And here we are, feuding in God's dressing room even before the curtain rises. Oh! –' He covered his face and fell into her lap, unable to say any more.

Instinctively Mapula fingered his hair. 'In God's dressing room,' she thought. 'What does he mean?' But his anguish stabbed at her heart. Trying to forget herself, she only sought within her a tenderness to quell the bitter wretchedness she had heard in his voice.

'Linga, no! Let me show you something else – something that I understand. It is no more so long before you and I can marry. I dream about the home that we are going to have. I … I want that home, Linga. You taught me that the woman's greatest contribution to civilisation so far has been to furnish homes where great men and great ideas have developed. Moreover, there's our problem. Let us rather think of ways of handling my father. No, no; not now. Let us think now of now.'

Thabo was running faster now that he was nearing home. His mind was in a whirl, but he knew that he had to tell his father. The lopsided gate was in the far corner, so he smartly leaped over the fence where it was slack. He stopped abruptly at the door. He always did when there were people. But now, he soon realised, these people were his two uncles – Uncle Alpheus and Uncle Frans. He knew how great news always brings a glory of prestige on the head of the bringer. Thabo felt himself almost a hero now, for these two men were diehard stalwarts in the Russian cause. Uncle Alpheus was a romantic firebrand. Uncle Frans was a scheming character of the power behind the throne variety. They were complementary to each other: together, a formidable team.

'Father, where is he?' hissed Thabo, breathing hard. The excitement in his voice aroused everyone.

'Holy Shepherd! What's the matter, boy?' cried Uncle Alpheus.

'Mapula, Mapula. She loves with a Letebele.'

'What!' exploded Uncle Alpheus. 'Where is she?' Then more calmly: 'Come'n, boy. Tell us everything more quietly; your father is out there?'

'J-J-Jonas t-t-tells me – J-Jonas is a boy who works with me – Jonas tells me that Mapula loves with a Letebele. They always meet at the hospital, but never in the sitting room. He hopes to marry her.'

'Never!' barked Alpheus.

Just then the door burst open. A party of men carried in the limp form of Thabo's father. He was unconscious and blood streamed all over his face. Beyond them, just outside the door, a crowd had gathered. Everyone was at once asking what had happened. As the news spread ugly moods swept the crowd. Ra-Thabo was carried into the bedroom and tended by the women. Alpheus and Frans returned to the foreroom and conferred.

'What now?' Alpheus asked Frans.

'Of course, we must revenge. You will talk to the people – the women. Talk fire into them. Connect it with the Mapula business; that'll warm them. Suggest drugs – a Letebele must use drugs, mustn't he. I'll be in the house. Just when they begin to get excited I'll arrange to carry Ra-Thabo out – to the hospital, you know. See if we can't get them bad!' he smiled cheerlessly.

Outside, the crowd – mostly women – was thickening. Even in the streets they could be seen coming along in groups, blanketed men and women. From the house Thabo and his little sister, Martha, joined the crowd. It was obvious that their uncles were going to do something about it.

Alpheus stepped on to the little mud wall. He raised his left hand and the blanket over it rose with it. That movement was most dramatic. In a few moments the crowd moved closer to him and became silent. Then he began to speak. He began in a matter of fact voice, giving the bare fact that Ra-Thabo, their leader, had been hurt. Warming gradually, he discussed the virtues of this man. Then he went on to tell of how this man had actually been hurt. Not confused fighting nor cowardly brutalities rose in the mind as this man spoke, but a glorious picture of crusaders charging on in a holy cause behind their lion-hearted leader. Oh, what a clash was there! The Matabele were pushed beyond Westbury Station. There the heroes met a rested, reinforced enemy. For a moment all that could be seen was the head of Ra-Thabo going down among them. The clang of battle could be heard, the furious charge could be seen, in the words of this man who was not there. The Basutos fought desperately and won so much ground that their all but lost leader could be rescued and carried back home. And what finds he there?

Alpheus's voice went down, softer and heavier, touching strings of pathos, rousing tragic emotions which the hearts present had never before experienced. There was an automatic movement in the crowd as everybody strained forward to hear. In awful, horror-filled whispers he told of Ra-Thabo's daughter giving herself to a Letebele. 'The thing is not possible!' he hissed. 'It would not have happened if the maid had not been bewitched with drugs. Are you going to brook it?' he cracked. 'No!' all the throats roared. 'Are you ready for vengeance?' 'Now!' thundered the mob. Someone in the crowd shouted 'Mule! Hit them!' Then the women took up their famous war cry, chilling to a stranger, but driving the last doubting spirit there to frenzy and fury.

Ee! – le! – le! – le! – le! – le! – le! –Eu! – Eu! – Eu!

Now they were prancing and swaying in uninterpretable rhythms. A possessed bard in their midst was chattering the praises of the dead, the living and the unborn, his words clattering like the drumsticks of a fiend.

'Let us go past Maraisburg and attack them from the rear!' yelled Alpheus over the din.

At that moment the door of the house went open. The mob which had been on the point of dashing out recoiled. The sight they saw stunned them. Frans and two other men were carrying out Ra-Thabo, besmeared with blood. Thabo saw Uncle Alpheus leaping with trailing blanket and yelling, 'To Maraisburg!' Again he leaped over the fence into the street. The mob followed hard on his heels.

As the last blanket swept round the corner, Frans turned back to the injured man. His two helpers had also been drawn in by the irresistible suction of mob-feeling. With a smile, he said to the unhearing Ra-Thabo: 'I'll have to get a taxi to take you to hospital, brother.' Then he carried him back into the house.

Late in the afternoon the train from Randfontein suddenly stopped at Maraisburg. Everybody was surprised. Something must be wrong. This train never stops at Maraisburg. Then suddenly!

'All change! All change!' And more brusquely: 'Come'n, puma! Puma! Out!'

Linga and Mapula hurried out. News had arrived that trouble had started again at Newclare, more seriously than usual. All trains from Randfontein were being stopped here and sent back.

Shrugging his shoulders, Linga drew Mapula away and arm in arm they strolled along the platform, out by the little gate, into some suburban area. For a time they walked on in silence. Then Mapula spoke.

'I hope I'll get back in time,' she said.

'Let's walk faster then. We might get a lift outside the

suburb.' They walked into the open country. Linga knew that if he could only find a certain golf course somewhere around here, he would know where the road was. Meanwhile, they had to stumble on over rough country and Mapula's cork-heel shoes were tormenting her toes. She limped on as stoically as she could. Linga did not notice her suffering as he was looking out for familiar landmarks. Those trees looked suspiciously like the golf course to him.

When they reached the trees Mapula said: 'Linga, let us rest here; my toes are suffering.'

'All right,' he replied. 'But I must look for the road. Let's look for a cool place where you may rest, while I search for the golf course.'

'Mm.'

He led her amongst the trees. She sat down and pulled off her shoes. When he thought he saw a shadow of distress flit across her brow, he bent down, took her hand, pressed it and then muttered: 'Back in a moment, sweet.' He rose slowly, looked at her indecisively, then turned away slowly and walked off.

He did not search far before he noticed a torn and faded flag. The hole was nearby. Suddenly he emerged from the cluster of trees and came across the road.

But his attention was caught by a horde of Russians pursuing a woman who came flying towards Linga. Should he chance it? He spoke fluent Sesotho and believed he could pass as a Mosotho, possibly as a Russian. He quickly drew a white handkerchief from his trouser pocket and tied it round his head. This made him, he knew, an active supporter of the Russian cause. Skirts flying, the woman sped past him. Facing the mob, he shouted: 'Helele! Hail!'

All its wrath spent, the mob crowded round out of sheer curiosity. Some were even in a jocular mood now, one playing lustily on a concertina. But here and there Linga could see deadly weapons, snatched up in their hasty exodus from Newclare. He spoke to them in fluent Sesotho, taking his idiom from Teyateyaneng. He asked if that was the road to Newclare; he said that he worked in Roodepoort, but was going to Newclare because his uncle there wanted more manpower in the house. Won't they please tell him where this road is?

'Che! It is no Letebele this; this is a child of at home,' remarked Alpheus.

'Kgele! You speak it, man,' said a burly fellow. Then everyone directed Linga how to get to Newclare.

As fate would have it, just then Mapula came running, shoes in hand and stockings twisted around her neck.

'Linga! Linga, darling mine! What are they doing to you?' she screamed, as she forced her way through the crowd. Linga stiffened. When she came to him she flung her arms around him and clung to him with all her strength, crying all the time.

Then she saw her uncle stupefied like the rest of them, standing there. She fled to him and begged him to save her lover. He pushed her aside and walked up to Linga. He stood before him, arms akimbo.

'Ehe! So you are a Letebele, after all. You lie so sleekly that I can understand why my niece thinks she loves you.' Then he swung round, his blanket trailing in an arc: 'Friends, we need go no further. This is the dog that bewitched my brother's child. Let's waste no time with him. Tear him to pieces!' The mob rushed upon Linga: 'Mmate! Mmate! Strike him!'

'Uncle! Uncle!' cried Mapula. But even as she cried she knew that nothing could be done. She had courted the contempt of her people, and she understood now that all her entreaties were falling upon deaf ears. Whether from convenience or superstition – it did not signify which – she was considered the victim of the Letebele's root-craft.

From the scuffling mob suddenly flew an axe which fell at her feet. In a flash she knew her fate. Love, frustrated beyond bearing, bent her mind to the horrible deed.

Mapula acted. Quickly she picked up the axe whilst the mob was withdrawing from its prey, several of them bespattered with blood. With the axe in her hand, Mapula pressed through them until she reached the inner, sparser group. She saw Alpheus spitting upon Linga's battered body. He turned with a guttural cackle – He-he-he! He-he-he! – into the descending axe. It sank into his neck and down he went. She stepped on his chest and pulled out the axe. The blood gushed out all over her face and clothing.

That evil-looking countenance she gradually turned to the stunned crowd, half lifting the axe and walking slowly but menacingly towards the largest group. They retreated – a hundred and twenty men and women retreated before this devil-possessed woman with the ghastly appearance.

But then she saw the mangled body of the man she loved and her nerve snapped. The axe slipped from her hand and she dropped on Linga's body, crying piteously: 'Jo-o! Jo-o! Jona-jo! Jo-na-jo!'

Someone came and lifted her up. Someone else was dragging Alpheus's bleeding corpse by the collar so that his shoes sprang out one after the other.

The crowd was going back now. All the bravado gone, they were quiet and sulky. Only the agonised wailing of Mapula. Every breast was quelled by a sense of something deeply wrong, a sense of outrage. The tumult in every heart, feeling individually now, was a human protest insistently seeking expression, and then that persistent wail of the anguished girl, torturing the innermost core of even the rudest conscience there.

The men felt themselves before God, the women heard the denunciations of thwarted love. Within they were all crying bitterly: 'Jo-o! Jo-o! Jo-nana-jo!'

The Nice Time Girl

'Damn it all, I'm going to the party,' Eunice Maoela finally said to herself, putting aside the crudely printed party ticket that Maggie Modise had given her in Prinsloo Street, Pretoria. She went into the bathroom to wash up, all the time worrying about her cruel lot. Theophilus Maoela, her forty-four-year-old husband, was 'too cold' for her and, in any case, he was away most of the time at his teaching post in faraway Phokeng outside Rustenburg, coming home rarely for weekends. And then her only son was staying with her mother in Pietersburg. She strode into her bedroom.

'Damn it all, I'm going.'

So she put on a sheath costume with a provocative slit along one leg and went to the party in Tladi Street, Atteridgeville. Right from the gate she flung herself into the party. She swayed her hips and slid her feet to the rhythms of the jive number. A Johannesburg jive sheik rudely left his partner and made for her.

'Baby,' he said, 'what you got don't matter; it's what you give – now, come on, give! Give! Give!' – snapping his fingers at each give and swaying his knees slowly.

She broke into her own ad lib, a complicated intertwinery of her legs that moved like the spokes of a spinning wheel. How did she manage it in that sheath costume? Maybe that's how that costume got its slit.

When the number ended the crowd that had stopped to watch them cheered. Eunice felt that she was once more in those reckless days before marriage. Her partner led her into the house and ordered two beers. They found a corner on a studio couch and talked, while some Lady Selborne boys crooned.

'I'm Matthew Modise from George Goch,' he said. 'Related to the Modises here. I came over with some Rand boys.'

He paused, waiting for her to introduce herself. But she was scared, now that the first wild fling was over. After all, Johannesburg boys are dangerous!

So he went on: 'I didn't expect Pretoria dames could jive like that. Baby, you're hot stuff!' His praise warmed her to him. The beer came endlessly to help break down her resistance.

Now and then they went to the veranda to jive, and when they did so the veranda was all theirs.

'Honey,' he said at length, 'let's blow to some cosy spot. This crowd just ain't private.'

'Come to my joint,' she said impulsively. She knew he was a playboy but she wanted to play a dangerous game.

'Sure it's safe?' he asked uneasily.

'Sure!'

At her home in Seiso Street she gave him a meal. That night Eunice told Matthew the story of her wretched marriage, of her husband's coldness and her loneliness.

'Look, Eunice,' Matthew said, 'how about chancing it with me?'

She was silent for a long time, so he argued feverishly: 'You don't see, the blues'll get you. Maybe not now, maybe not tomorrow, but they'll get you right enough. And then you'll grab any worm that comes along. It ain't gonna be me, it ain't gonna be no guy you go for, cos you're just gonna be goddam desperate. Me too, I'm gonna go to pieces, thinkin of you, and maybe just snatch any tart that comes my way. An two lives'll be busted.'

'If only he'd do a wicked thing,' she sobbed. 'If only I could catch him drunk or with another woman ... but you don't walk out on a man just like that ... Moreover, Matthew, there's my boy – '

'I don't mind, darling,' he misunderstood her. 'I gotta boy myself.'

'Mm-mm, that's not the point,' she replied. 'I'm afraid if my husband can prove that I'm not a fit person to raise the kid, I'll lose it.'

The following morning when he left Matthew said, 'Here's my address in case you want me.'

She looked him straight in the face and said, 'My boy means more to me than nice times.'

But for the whole of the following week Eunice felt that she had missed a lifetime's opportunity to escape. She felt defeated. What was worse, Theophilus came home that weekend. The contrast between this tame, genial husband and her vivacious jive king stood out roughly. She knew one taste made her hunger for more of the forbidden fruit, had even at the price of a wicked crime.

On the Monday after Theophilus had left she went to George Goch. Only after painting the city red for three days did she return to Atteridgeville.

Three weeks later Theophilus Maoela was quietly reading in his sitting room. He had arrived the evening before.

It was a Saturday morning and his wife had just returned from the post office to send a wire to someone or other. Now she was busy in the kitchen, preparing the midday meal. The thought crossed his mind that his wife might be lonely, what with the long periods he stayed away, and the fact that he was too tired or busy to give her a good time. He thought it over for a long time.

Then at table he spoke. 'My dear,' he said, 'couldn't we visit your ma in Lady Selborne some time this afternoon? It's so lonely here.'

What a lame attempt to cheer up this bleak life, she thought. But aloud she said: 'I want to be with you, dear ... alone with you. Tell you what, let's take a long walk this evening. Perhaps we'll rediscover the old magic of our love.' So sweetly she said that, the husband sighed, 'Ah – '

But before their evening walk, Eunice had to go out again.

Husband and wife walked out of the location into the

grassveld beyond the main road. Out of sight they held hands, and chewed stalks, and didn't even think of snakes in the grass.

But suddenly out of the tall grass leapt four or five strange, evil-looking men on Eunice's side. She screamed, but the shock must have been too sudden for her voice to go far.

Theophilus sprang to her defence and when the attack struck he fought with bare hands. But the odds were too great for him and he was clubbed unconscious.

Then the butchers stabbed him to death in cold, greasy blood. After that, gloved hands went through his pockets and turned them inside out, but found only small change. The motive looked like robbery.

A few minutes later a car roared away.

'But why didn't you run for help, Mrs Maoela? We could've cordoned off the car in a few minutes.'

'When they struck him down, I fainted.'

'Yes, I see that. Can you describe any of the attackers?'

'It was dim ... darkening twilight ... and I fainted too soon ...'

Detective Mphahlele bit his nails, frowning pensively. The trouble is that the hoodlums acted too swiftly. Then that car. The mark it left on the hard road had been blurred by other car tracks. Then the spot. The motive was obviously robbery. But who was so stupid as to go lie in tall grass to rob people at a place where people rarely passed, only motorists flying along at breakneck speed? The detective cursed all unmethodical criminals.

Then he tried the angle of Mrs Maoela's answers. Barren answers! They were such a dead end that he chose to think of the pretty Mrs Maoela herself. Yes, lovely woman that! But she looked lonely. Anyway, who wouldn't look down when her nearest relation had just been brutally murdered. Ah, yes! A murder. That's the job. Must get back to the answers ...

He racked his brain for a solution until sheer fatigue made

him numb in the head and he found he wasn't thinking any more. Just spinning round and round in a dizzy nightmare. He decided to sleep on it. And the following day he would study the reports of the other men on the case.

'I'll try to let you know now and then, Mrs Maoela, how things are shaping,' he said, as he rose to go out. But from the way he walked it seemed clear that he didn't expect things to take any sensible shape at all.

'Philip! Philip! Wake up, wake up,' Mrs Mphahlele shook her husband huddled up beneath the warm blankets. It was a matter of urgency.

He stirred and moaned. Then one eye popped open.

'Philip, Constable Mushi is here to see you. He says it's urgent and he must talk to you personally.'

Detective Mphahlele crept out of the warm nest and, still in his pyjamas, stumbled on to go and see the constable.

'Yes, Darkie, what's up?' Then he yawned.

Constable Mushi spoke carefully. 'Five fellows from Joburg have been caught with a stolen car last night. They had no stolen goods with them, no liquor, no dagga, no nothing. But a big bloodstained butcher knife was found in the car. Commandant Joubert wants you to come to the police station immediately.'

'I see,' said the now fully awake Detective Mphahlele. 'Well, let me get ready to go.'

Eunice received Detective Mphahlele with dumbfounded panic.

'Do not be afraid, Mrs Maoela. I've only come to fulfil a promise. I told you that I'd let you know how things are shaping.'

Her throat felt dry and sour.

He took his time with her, though. 'My dear Mrs Maoela, it's really terrible how these Johannesburg criminals think that Pretoria is a pushover. It hurts my pride. Some day we've got to teach them a thorough lesson ...'

Eunice found the suspense excruciating. 'Mphahlele! Do you not realise that my husband is dead; that I'm not interested in a policeman's pride. I expect you to arrest the murderers!'

He sighed. 'Yes, Mrs Maoela, I've got to get the murderers – *all* of them. Let me tell you how far we've got. Last night a speed-cop stopped a Johannesburg car on the Pretoria-Johannesburg road for overspeeding and reckless driving. He found that it was a car stolen three days ago in Johannesburg. The fellows in the car tried something funny, but the speed-cop had a partner close by. They were brought back to Pretoria. Mrs Maoela, in that car we found a heavy bloodstained hunting knife. It didn't take much questioning to get the truth out of them. We have methods, Mrs Maoela, very persuasive methods, Mrs Maoela.

'Now four of those fellows are hardened criminals, well known at Marshall Square – you know that's the main Johannesburg police station. They have also spent long stretches in the Fort, Johannesburg's jail. But one fellow hasn't a record at all. Of course, there hasn't been much time to check up as yet. But the others said that it was he who bought them for the killing. Strangely enough, he claims that a woman bought *him*.

'Well, we know cornered rats will always try to shift the blame on others. We wanted proof. He said proof could be found in a telegram this woman sent him, making the appointment for the murder of your husband. The police in Johannesburg are searching his room in George Goch for the telegram. We also want to find out if it is true that many people in George Goch can testify that he and this woman were friends ... Intimate friends, Mrs Maoela.'

Eunice couldn't take any more. 'Yes, I did it! I did it! Life with my husband had become intolerable!' she shouted hysterically.

That night Detective Mphahlele asked his wife, 'I wonder why Beauty sometimes becomes the Beast?'

Forbidden Love

Dora Randolph was now running in the dark down the road that dipped into the hollow of the bridge spanning the stream that separated Noordgesig from the Western Areas. From the bridge the road climbed the hillock and sailed away to Newclare, Western Township and Sophiatown.

He must have seen her, for his dark form swam towards her and caught her in his strong arms.

'Not here, darling,' he said hastily, 'some car lights may strike upon us.'

He led her higher up the road, off it, into the tall grass.

Suddenly she caught his coat lapels and dragged him down so that no one could see them. He clambered towards her and curled her into his arms. His lips thrilled upon hers, burning sweet, and with digging fingertips she tried to find the source of his fire in his spinal column.

Then the flames went out of them, settling into a low glow. She broke away with a sigh. She caught a stalk, put it in her mouth and turned to look at the scattered lights of Noordgesig.

'They were at it again, Sweetie,' she said between her teeth, 'and what makes me mad is I cannot argue back any more.'

'What did they say now?' Mike asked, a little worried.

'That Mr Van Vuuren was at home. It looked almost as if Dad had called him in to preach to us. He spoke about how it is terribly important that we keep away from the "Natives", otherwise we would be associated with them. And his voice had a trick of making that word "associated" sound horrible. But what made me hate him is the way he stared at Louisa as he spoke. I –'

'Louisa is that sister of yours who is dark, isn't she?' Michael

Chabakeng asked. He had seen her once at the Rhythmic Cinema with Dora and he remembered how she was darker, even than he, and she had woolly, kinky hair like his.

Dora went on: 'Yes, the dark one, and I feel like giving them all the hurt back that they make little Louisa suffer. Why wasn't it I, Mike? Why wasn't I dark, instead of fair? Then you might not have been so afraid of my love?'

'Huh?' Michael was so taken aback by the sudden tenseness in her tone that he did not quite know what to say.

She turned her head and placed her chin on to his chest. 'Somehow, Mike,' she tried to explain, softened again now, 'I feel trapped by a doubly guilty shame. I am ashamed that it is my people who are in the forefront of every move against your people – ashamed of my father whom I love, but who is violent in his hatred of Africans; ashamed of my sister Louisa, who ought to feel nearer your people but hates them so unreasonably; ashamed of my brother's shame for having been classified as an African; ashamed of my mother's silence when I suspect (I know it!) that she disapproves of their attitudes. And then, Sweetie, sometimes when I listen to them all, I – I – I am ashamed, in a queer way that I hate, of this secret love of ours. Oh!'

Michael drew her close and then his voice came, softly as if it came out of the grass: 'I don't know if I can make you understand this. But, darling, everybody's trouble is that he is afraid. *Everybody!* Even you and I. Your father, and that … that Mr Van Vuuren are afraid their old world is turning over and they will now have to fight for things. And they are not used to fighting. They have too long … too long …' He searched frantically for words that would not hurt her and at last he said weakly, 'Too long not fought.'

'Yes, Mike,' she said.

'Your sister, Louisa, is afraid because of this thing that might tear her away from you – all whom she loves, and from the comparative safety of your way of life; this thing, this business of becoming an African is nearest to her, seems would soonest catch her in its cruel fingers. More than the fear of your father and Mr Van Vuuren, hers is most likely to become cruel.'

Michael thought about what he was saying for a moment. The significance of his own words was only just becoming clear even to himself.

'But my mother, Mike – I can't understand her silence.'

'I'm not sure I can understand everybody's fear,' Michael said after a moment, 'but tell me: haven't you ever felt that your mother chose silence because she doesn't want to say anything that might influence you children?'

'I see, Mike,' Dora said, feeling with her fingers for the hard swelling on his biceps, 'and my fear is that I know I'm doing just the thing that my mother fears her words might influence us children into doing, too.'

'Partly. But, my dear, let's forget all the world's fear. Let's forget even your fear and mine. Between you and me there is, lying side by side with the fear, a faith. Let's feed the faith. Let's talk of love.'

'No, Sweetie, let's not talk of love, let's just lie still in each other's arms and feel it.'

After a long while he released her, raised her to her feet. 'Tomorrow, three o'clock show at the Rhythmic. Here's your ticket.' He kissed her again.

The headlights of a car on a bend higher up shone on them for a moment. A ghost-like shadow flew out to Noordgesig like a tongue flicked out of a mouth mockingly.

As the driver of the car dipped into the bowl towards the river and the bridge, he said to his companions: 'That guy sure must have a dangerous weapon.'

In their two-room apartment in Sophiatown Michael was again nagging his sister about the one thing that was eating into his peace of mind.

'You keep stalling, dodging me, but do you think it is really in the best interests of the child that you hide its name? After all, I've been thinking of getting married myself … some time soon ...' and his voice trailed away.

'Don't you worry, Mike,' his sister Salome said, 'I've the child's true interests at heart. But there are times when there is good reason for not doing the obvious thing. I assure you the child's father is an honourable man. That is all I can say for the moment. You must trust me.'

Michael looked into the fire in the stove, his mouth twisted into a strained grimace of concentrated thinking.

'I still don't like it,' he said at length. 'What about you, what about your future? However romantic, I don't like the picture of a man who will not stand up to his responsibilities.'

'You don't understand.' And she went on humming one of those catchy songs that attack the streets of Sophiatown now and then for a brief spell.

Michael felt beaten again. He was always beaten in this game. The trouble was that he had full confidence in his sister's intelligence. But this, she was right, he could not understand. He remembered something he had heard somewhere: 'A woman in love is operating at the lowest level of the intellect.' He went out.

Meneer Careels of the Noordgesig Primary School leaned over the gate of the school yard and looked for the small group of Coloured boys who would be sitting in a circle at a corner of the yard. He called one of them.

'Take my bag and put it into the History classroom,' he said to the sandy-haired, smart-looking youngster who came up to him. He looked at the circle of boys wistfully. He knew what they were doing now during these precious few minutes before the school started. They were teasing each other in the age-old school tradition. 'Probably vulgar, the naughty little scamps,' he thought tolerantly as his mind went back to his own schooldays as a youngster. Then he hurried away to Aunt Sannie's house for that daily cup of coffee.

Meanwhile Freddie Williams, the sandy-haired, smart-looking youngster he had sent, sped across the playground to the History classroom. Freddie was not going to miss that morning's session of their little tease-club. But gee! They got Bobby Randolph at last. Freddie had met Dick Peters that morning on their way to school and that eternal victim of Bobby Randolph's tease-tongue had intimated to Freddie that he had a bombshell with which he was going to blow Bobby to bits and blazes. That is why, as he went flying over the playground, Freddie had shouted to the gang already assembled, 'Wait for me!'

Dick Peters did wait for Freddie. He wanted a full audience and he wanted to make sure that his friend Freddie was present in case of any fighting.

Freddie was still gasping for breath when Dick stood up, faced Bobby and exploded his bombshell without finesse or ceremony.

'Your Sissy goes with a Naytif!' Dick said.

'You lie!'

'Yes, it's true. I seen her by the bioscope on Saturday. Your Sissy goes with a Naytif!'

Then the gang burst into laughter. Bobby broke loose with such a fierce barrage of blows upon Dick that they both tumbled over into the playground. Dick did not stand a chance. Bobby's arms were flailing into his face and the blood was spurting out. Dick yelled out with sudden fear and pain.

Meneer Careels had to push aside the cheering youngsters before he could get at the rolling figures. He pulled Bobby off and held the two apart.

'What're you fighting for?'

'He hit me first,' Dick said inconsequentially.

'Why did you hit him, Bobby?'

'He says my sister goes with a Naytif!'

'It's true,' Dick shouted, 'I seen them myself on Saturday by the bioscope.'

For a moment Meneer Careels was stunned by the news. Through his mind rushed with painful vividness the picture of his proposal of marriage to Dora Randolph and the disdainful rejection she had given him. He could see again her lip curling up in contempt. He knew ... he had always known, that she rejected him because of his drinking habits that were notorious in the township, but he felt hurt too deep to admit his weakness.

Suddenly his own lip curled up as a malicious thought darted through his mind.

'To the head you go, both of you,' he said as he dragged them away.

After Mr Phillips had taken in the whole story he sent the youngsters off, asking them to report back at 'half past one', when the school went out. He told Meneer Careels to wait a moment as he wanted to talk to him.

'Meneer,' began the head with a pained expression in his eyes, 'it is our duty to hush up the whole cruel affair. You know, we could handle the youngsters, and the matter need not go further than this school.'

'But ... but ...'

'Yes?'

'But I think we owe it to the girl's family to tell them of the danger their daughter is putting them in.' Meneer Careels was most sanctimonious.

Mr Phillips stared at the lean man before him long and hard before he spoke.

Then he said: 'Of course, our interest is just for the good and safety of the family. We do not have' – with deep emphasis – 'any desire to do them harm. It would not somehow mysteriously happen that the whole world knows of it.'

'Really, I must say!' was all that Meneer Careels could manage.

Then both men stared silently out of the window. It was a long minute before Mr Phillips could say, 'That will be all, Meneer.'

But it did somehow mysteriously happen that the whole world came to know of it. Dora's disgrace was on everybody's lips.

To everybody, except to Dora herself, this was disaster. She decided that it was release from the long months of stolen, forbidden love. And there was a thrill in defiance.

This, of course, gave added fuel to the wagging tongues. Said somebody in the bus in her father's presence, 'I learn the brazen hussy doesn't care at all. It just goes to show the government isn't exactly wrong in all cases that it reclassifies back to Kaffir.' The old man winced.

And added fuel to the rising tempers. Dora's brother Davie got together a few of his friends who solemnly pledged themselves: 'Wait till we catch him.'

So even if Michael had seen the group of Coloured lads near the doorway of the Rhythmic Cinema that Saturday, he would not have suspected a thing.

He had decided to take it easy with Dora since he had received her hurried note that the whole thing had cracked despite her insistence that she didn't care a damn. He had written her that for some time, at least, they would have to go to the cinema separately.

But this was a great picture. He had read about it in the papers. So he just had to see it. He knew that Dora was going to be there, but he hoped she would be sensible.

Then he saw a group of African fellows gesticulating and arguing heatedly with the manager of the cinema. He went up to them and found, dash it all! – the film was banned to 'Children under Twelve and Natives'.

Suddenly he heard a voice shouting. 'Aw, beat up the blerrie Kaffirs!' As he swung round, a Coloured chap caught him by the shoulder and hit him in the mouth, cutting his upper lip.

'Davie don't!' came Dora's shriek from somewhere and Michael knew that he had had it.

She appeared before him and faced her brother.

His eyes spread wide. 'So this is the blerrie bastard! Hi, boys, this is Dora's Kaffir!'

They ignored the other Africans who scampered away in all directions and crowded in upon Michael and Dora. Dora quickly said to Michael in a fierce whisper, 'I'm with you in this till the end.'

As they got near, Michael pushed Dora behind him and faced Davie.

'Look, Davie boy,' he said tautly, 'take my advice and don't do it. I'm not scared of being beaten up. I'm scared of what this will mean. Take my advice and don't do it.'

'Yefies!' said Davie, 'what does he think he can do – nothing!'

Suddenly he kicked Michael in the stomach so that he doubled up. Someone caught hold of Dora and held her fast. The others jumped upon Michael and attacked him with a mad fury. He made no attempt to fight back. Only instinctively he protected his face as best he could.

Then someone blew a police whistle and the attackers dashed into the maze of byways and alleys of Fordsburg. But Michael was out like a dead cinder.

When he came to, Dora was weeping over him. He tried to lift himself but could not. She helped him up, still crying bitterly. Together they staggered to the bus stop, off to Sophiatown.

At home Michael fainted again. So Dora had to explain to his sister what had happened. She introduced herself and then told the story straightforwardly.

A queer look came into sister Salome's face, something like amusement.

'Randolph? Randolph? Randolph, you say? And your brother's name is Davie. David Randolph. I got an idea. You stay here and as soon as Mike is well enough, we'll go and see old Davie, nè?'

For days Salome did not speak about the matter. The two women who loved Michael so much looked after him, nursed him back to health.

Then one Sunday morning Salome suddenly said: 'Look, you two, I think it's time that we went to see old Davie. I want a little talk with him.'

'Aw, cut it out, I don't want any more trouble,' said Michael.

'Oh no, there won't be trouble at all. Just a little talk,' Salome replied mysteriously.

Dora guided them to her home, her heart beating wildly. They found her whole family at lunch. Even Mr Van Vuuren was there, philosophising expansively. Davie went pale.

Before they could say anything Salome took over.

'Hello, Davie,' she began, 'remember me? You beat up my brother because he's in love with your sister. Okay, now I've brought my brother to beat you up because you were in love with *his* sister. Fair enough.'

'You lie!' Davie said hoarsely.

'I thought you'd say that, so I brought some proof. Where do you suppose I got this handsome picture of yours, Davie? And just in case you deny that one too, I'd like your father to read these flaming letters you once wrote to me.'

She pushed a neatly tied bundle of letters to the old man, saying tartly, 'And to think I treasured these letters because they came from the only man I ever loved.'

The old man seemed only then to be suddenly galvanised into life. 'Get out! Get out of my house!' he shrieked.

Salome kept cool.

'Oh no you don't. If you get tough I'll take your son to court for not supporting his child for the last three years. Mike, you've been asking me all the time who the father of my child is and I've been silent. I told you it's a man I love, a man who would come into the open if he could but that his circumstances were exceptional. You thought it was a married man. Well, that is the man!' – pointing a trembling finger at Davie.

The whole family was stunned. Salome was now heaving with emotion.

The old man grabbed the packet of letters and said, 'You can't prove it.'

Salome laughed out loud, a hard, cruel laugh.

'There's one letter at home, the one in which your son

begged me not to expose him.'

Then Dora's mother spoke out. 'My grandchild! I've got a grandchild. My God, I must see that child.'

Something in the old lady's voice calmed Salome.

'Yes, mother,' she said softly.

Michael and Dora walked out quietly. She looked into his eyes and said: 'Somehow I think the fear will fade away now.'

Marta

The people in the queue stood drearily with an air of defeated waiting over them. Sophiatown on Monday mornings is like that. An anticlimax after Sunday's excesses.

Then Marta came along, still drunk. Her baby was hanging dangerously on her back as she staggered up Victoria Road. Somebody in the queue remarked dryly: 'S'funny how a drunk woman's child never falls.'

'Shet up!' said Marta in the old, vulgarest word she knew.

She stood swaying a moment on her heels and watched the people in the queue bitterly. A bus swung round the Gibson Street corner and narrowly missed her. Three or four women in the queue screamed: 'Oooo!' But Marta just turned and staggered off into Gibson Street. The child lurched on her back.

There was no gate to the yard in Gibson Street, because there was no fence to make a gate into. So Marta just walked up to the house. She toed the door open and just then, feeling that she was going to feel sick, dived for the unmade bed. The child nearly shot out of the pocket on Marta's back. It started crying, but Marta just said: 'Shet up.'

A tall African whose complexion was five minutes to midnight turned round from the mirror, his hands arrested around a half-made tieknot. He had a shock of hair on his head and it made him look like a tall golliwog. But in his eyes the anger crept like the backsplash of the tide. His upper lip curled, showing a flash of the whitest teeth.

When he spoke it was a sort of snarl. ' 'Strue's God, Marta,' he growled with that abrupt accent of the Rhodesians, 'one of these days I go to chock you tille you die. I'll teash you to stop drinking and for to start looking after your house – ' And just as if to make his point, he stepped into a plate with dry morsels of food that crunched under his weight. 'Agh, sis!' he hissed.

'Aw, shet up, man!'

For a moment he stood there and stared at her in stark, stupid fury. Then suddenly he was galvanised into action. He leapt at her and grabbed her by the throat, squeezing, squeezing ...

What's the use of fretting? Life is too large for that. And life must be lived – sweetly or bitterly – but always intensely. It is like a burning log that crackles at every knot and explodes in little bursting pellets of fire. The pain or the slow creeping sorrow. The sudden fear of dark location alleys. The shifting aside to avoid the attention of young hooligans who sit and swear on the shop corners. Then the wild, fire-mad midnight parties. Getting drunk. It comes on you in fumes, thick folds of smoke that trap you and cloud you. And suddenly, illogically, the police! The police! The police! What's the use? You carry a dangerous weapon, the police get you. You go without one, the tsotsis get you. But it is nice to have a woman, your woman, made yours by the long moment of fierce love and the close embrace, tighter, tighter, tighter ...

Until a child cries in sudden panic!

Jackson realised with a shock what he was doing. Had he killed Marta? O God! What had he done? He saw all the tawdry, vulgar, violent recklessness of their lives. Something just keeps coming off wrong in this hit and run mislife. And it's not so much Marta's drinking or his adulteries ... It's – it's – it's, well, damnitall!

Then Marta stirred and coughed. She tried to rise but found that she could not. Hoarsely she said to Jackson: 'The child, the child.' He saw where she had pinned him down with her body. He lifted her and pulled out the child. Then he stood there looking at Marta and the child anxiously. He felt they needed care ... but then a man's got to go to work.

You do anything, but you go to work. The police arrest

you by mistake; you do your all to get out, because you got to go to work. You pay Admission of Guilt. You admit anything, anything! So long as you go to work. But sometimes you got to go to jail. Then you go. It does not matter. Almost everybody you know has been to jail.

But then that long queue of men you had seen at your place of work, looking for work ...

Outside in the street, Jackson saw two little girls just suddenly breaking into a dance. For the sheer swing of it! He thought of how well Marta could do it.

Marta lay quietly for some time. Her throat was smarting, but her head was whirling less dizzily now. Then she reached out for the child and dragged it across her body. It felt like trying to hoist yourself up by tugging at your socks. Made it.

She examined the child carefully. It looked all right. It was gurgling now. She put it down on the bed again. Sleep came jaggedly.

When she woke, first it sounded like wild yelling. Then she saw them shouting at her to come and get up. Sophia was there, Emily and Boet Mike. They were nice. But Marta's head was still clanging. Drink does that to you when it rushes out.

'Come-ahn,' said Emily. 'Boet Mike's ship is in and Sophia stands all right. He-e-e, Boet Mike say, a bottle of straight! Sophia says, straight! Boet Mike says, straight! We said, no, let's get Marta first. Come-ahn, Marta.'

Marta hesitates. 'Jackson will kill me.'

Sophia looked as if she had never heard anything that funny. 'Since when have you been scared of Jackson?'

'All right,' Marta yielded, 'but let me first find Pulani to look after the child.'

But Sophie insisted that they go to her favourite shebeen in Gerty Street, because her husband who had got the shakes does not go there. Not ever. Of course, Marta did not like the woman of the house in Gerty Street. She puts on such airs since she's got her new radiogram. But it's not every day that Boet Mike's ship is in and that Sophia stands right.

The house in Gerty Street was a veranda, then a room, then a room again, then a back veranda. The first room was a combined sitting room and bedroom. The second one combined dining room and kitchen. They went into the sitting room bedroom.

Somebody in the dining room kitchen was practising jazz solos on a set of drums. But Marta and company did not mind.

Boet Mike said, 'Straight.' And they bought a bottle of brandy that looked like guilty blood. They drank from the bottle at first slowly, Emily serving into all sorts of glasses. She managed to serve an equal shot each time, because she measured the drink by her fingers on one glass, and from that glass she would serve all the others.

And the drum was raving on relentlessly. It was as if the drummer himself was getting drunker ahead of them.

The bottle went down slowly, but before it reached its ankles, Sophia who stood right said, 'Straight!'

Suddenly Marta sprang up and jived to the rhythms of the rumbling drums. The others chanted out for her. Marta's arms went out before her, her legs spread, her knees sagged, her eyes drooped and her mouth opened a little, and she moved forward in a shuffle, like a creature drawn irresistibly, half-consciously, to its doom. She shuffled towards the dining room kitchen.

The others followed her. In the other room the furniture had been moved aside and in one corner a young man, surely not eighteen yet, was beating the drums as though he wanted to work something evil out of him.

He suddenly broke into a rapid roll of raw rhythm. His arms were flailing in and out, so fast that they blurred. Marta was caught in the wild bursts like a loose fish and chips paper churned up in a sudden gust of wind. She leapt up, and when she landed again her feet sprinkled about in an intricate tracery. Then just as suddenly her feet stopped, so suddenly that the shock still shivered through the rest of her body.

Infinitely minute tremblings.

The drummer was watching her now. Their positions were reversed. It was she who was giving him direction now. She was transmitting the wild energy, with clenched teeth and open hands, creeping towards him. Her every sudden movement tore a roar from the drums.

Then abruptly she stopped and the cymbals clanged!

Marta sank tiredly into a chair. She felt that she had come back from somewhere, had committed something before which her spirit had often quailed. She didn't want to dance again or drink any more. She looked at the boy behind the drums. He seemed very shy, very young. Could he, could he really be that innocent, even after this thing he and she had done together?

He rose and started to go out, but Sophia, quite drunk now, would have none of it.

'Uh-uh, man, brother,' she drawled, 'don't go yet. Come with us, man. We stand right.'

He hesitated, looked towards Marta shyly. She looked at Sophia. She knew Sophia wanted him for herself, but then she knew Sophia and didn't like it. Somehow she felt this boy should not be dragged into their company. There was something about him that she felt with stupid stubbornness should be left intact.

'Come here, man, brother, come to Sophie.'

'No!' Marta was surprised at the violence of her own voice.

Sophia giggled. 'So, you want him. Well, I don't carredamn. You're a friend of mine, see?'

Marta caught the boy by the sleeve of his floral shirt. 'Let's get away from here! Quick!' The urgency in her voice impelled him.

Boet Mike said how about finishing off another straight, but she didn't wait to reply.

Outside Marta realised that she was drunker than she had thought. She looked up into the young man's face and tried to smile. 'Looks like you've got to take me home,' she said.

He gave her a look of sheerest adoration. It stung her to the softest centre. 'Look here, kid, I want you to promise me one thing. Promise me that you will never drink.'

'But I don't drink,' he protested.

'Still, promise me that you will never drink.'

A flash of anger showed in his face. 'You think I'm a kid, hey?'

'Nnnnoooooo,' she said thoughtfully. 'I don't mean just drinking. I mean don't go rough.'

He was shy again. So she said, 'Okay. Take me home. I'll try to explain there.'

'Honestly, Sophia, I didn't think that the explanation would take that long ... all day. I didn't know that we were at my place so long. All I know is that Jackson suddenly returned home. It was hopeless ... I could see from his eyes that he thought I was revenging for what had happened that morning. But I couldn't do it! I couldn't do it with that boy.

'Maybe it's true I was fed up with Jackson. Maybe I did want in my heart to make Jackson feel that other men could like me. But not with that boy, Sophia. Not with that boy.

'Now the people say, no case at all. No case at all because he was in my own house. In Jackson's own house, and Jackson had a right to kill him. But there's nothing that he did.'

Sophia felt for a moment like laughing lecherously. But somehow she just couldn't. She just couldn't.

Softly she asked: 'But you loved that boy, didn't you?'

Marta looked up through her tears. She looked at Sophia long before she decided that Sophia might understand.

Then just: 'Yes. The drunk woman's child has fallen.'

Henry Nxumalo

One Saturday afternoon Henry Nxumalo, the news editor of *The Golden City Post*, set out to Sophiatown to look for me. He didn't find me in. He came three times, but still didn't find me in. Curse my roving ways! Then he went to see another reporter friend, Bloke Modisane, and chatted with him into the early evening. Bloke thought that it was getting late, what with the boys outside becoming so knife happy these days, and he urged Henry to go home early or just to put up for the night. But Henry explained that he had a job to do in Newclare and proposed to go and sleep at his cousin Percy Hlubi's house in Western Township. So at about seven o'clock in the evening Henry left the 'Sunset Boulevard' – Bloke's home in Sophiatown – and went to Western Township, across the rails.

He must have felt disgracefully dry, because those days just after Christmas were arid, desert-like in the Western Areas. A man just couldn't find a drop. Henry got to Percy's house and explained to Percy and his wife that he would like to pass the night there. However, he would first like to go to Newclare where he had a job to do. He would return later to sleep. Meanwhile, the men sat talking whilst the woman prepared a bed for Henry. Before she turned in for the night, she told Henry that when he came back he would probably find them asleep. He shouldn't bother to knock; just open the door and go to your bed.

Percy looked at the time and noticed that it was close on eleven. He told Henry to postpone his trip to Newclare for the following day. It was so awfully late. 'Never put off for tomorrow what you can do today,' Henry backfired grinningly. Then he rose and walked out into the warm night. He never came back to the bed prepared for him.

The following morning Mrs Hlubi rose early to go to work in Krugersdorp. She was a nurse there and she normally took her train at Westbury Station. She set out for work at about a quarter past five that Sunday morning. When she got to the spot where Malotane Street flowed out of Ballenden Avenue like a tributary, she noticed a body lying on the green grass, one shoe off, one arm twisted behind it, the head pressed against the ground, the eyes glazed in sightless death. And bloody wounds all over the head and body. Good heavens, it was Henry Nxumalo!

In hysterical frenzy she rushed back home to tell her husband. Percy went to the scene and saw the battered body of his cousin. He got his friend, Mr Vil Nkomo, to inform Henry's employer. He contacted the police. He chartered a car to go and tell Henry's wife – most cheerless of tasks. Then he got someone to go round and tell all the *Drum* boys.

The way I got the news was through the wife of Benjamin Gwigwi Mrwebi. Gwigwi himself was away in Durban with his combo, the Jazz Dazzlers. So Salome, his wife, took it upon herself to inform those of us who were around. She found me still in bed, lazing luxuriously after eight o'clock, and she broke the news to me. Stunned, I crawled out of bed and went with her to the spot marked X. There was already a little crowd gathered and from all the streets flowing into Ballenden Avenue people were streaming to the spot.

There he lay, the great, gallant Henry Nxumalo who had fought bravely to bare cruelty, injustice and narrow-mindedness; there he lay in the broiling sun, covered by two flimsy rags.

He who had accepted the challenge of life and dedicated himself against the wrongs of mankind now lay on the roadside, his last battlefield the gutter, his last enemies the arrant knaves for whom, even, Henry had raised his trumpet call. And there was a staggering trail of bloody footsteps that told the graphic story of that night's drama. Let us read as best we can the story told in meandering blood.

About a hundred yards from Coronation Hospital there is a little gate. Less than ten yards from that gate is a pool of blood. The first sign of violence. From that pool footsteps made in blood turn in and out towards Western Township, showing how a man, mortally wounded, struggled with his great, unyielding spirit to get away. Twenty yards of agonised staggering and the man dropped off the road among the stones. Probably heaving, breathing heavily, he dragged himself up and struggled on ... and on ... and on. And the lifeblood spurts from him. Ah, a little patch of green grass, barely visible. Here might a man rest his gashed body. And he dropped.

But the strength ebbed out of him, drip-drip out of him. He must have fought madly with his heart when he thought of his unfinished work: that book about South Africa he was writing for America – the draft completed, but who could be trusted to give it the final polish? Florence, the wife who had always so patiently waited for him when he was out on his perilous escapades: who would care for her and her children? And that brotherhood of *Drum* men, who will continue to give them guidance and encouragement? And the life went out of him. So died Henry Nxumalo, 'Mr Drum'. Death is lonely even if your dear ones are there to hold a tender hand on your forehead. Death is desolate if you meet it far away from home on the roadside.

And meanwhile the butchers were somewhere wiping off their knives and probably cracking coarse jokes. It was 'Murder most foul, as in the best it is, But this most foul, strange and unnatural'.

When I started the column 'Us: Can Says' in *The Golden City Post* I dreamt of it as a forthright, hard-hitting, straight from the shoulder article, and I tried to make it so. But I had to go full-time on *Drum*.

I could not have been happier that it went into the hands of Henry Nxumalo, for me one of the best journalists that this country has produced. What he gave that column was humour, humanity and honesty.

He called it 'Lowdown', made it the most forthright, hard-hitting, straight from the shoulder, humorous, humane and honest column that has ever gone into ink. That was because he was Henry Nxumalo, the newspaper man who knew that 'you gotta get a story, boy. I like nonsense, but I like common sense more.'

And he lived for his people.

In this particular moment, after he has been brutally butchered, probably by the same men he lived and died for, I suspect he would like to say: 'Crime is the gravest evil of our day. See what I mean!'

And his tragic death would be sufficient testimony.

But the unknowing still ask, who was this Henry Nxumalo?

Henry was born thirty-nine years ago in Port Shepstone. His grandfather, Gqobo, was an ordinary tribal Zulu who died by falling over a cliff. His father, Lazarus, married a traditional Zulu girl, Josephine, and they had seven children: Henry, the eldest; Gertie, now late; the twins Benjamin, now living in Port Shepstone, and Daniel, now late; then Zebbar, also known as Lance, now living in Edenvale; Abigail, late, and Ntombizodwa, also late.

Because their parents died when they were still young, they more or less had to look after themselves. This one fact accounts for the independent spirit in Henry and his surviving brothers. Henry went to school at St Francis, Mariannhill, and did his Junior Certificate, but as he was doing Matric his father died and he had to abandon school. He took up a job as a kitchen boy in Durban, but left it because he didn't like it. He came to Johannesburg. He found a job in a boilermaker's shop. In his spare time he wrote poetry for *Bantu World*.

Later he got a job with *Bantu World* as a messenger and hung on for three years until he became sports editor. When the war came he joined up and became a sergeant. He went up North and made various friends. The world beyond showed him how other people thought and lived, so when he came back he was a frustrated man. He came back to *Bantu World* and made extra money by writing for a Negro paper, *The Pittsburgh Courier*. In 1946 he married the young nurse called Florence. He left to work on a gold mine, later did welfare work for the British Empire Service League and still freelanced for European papers. At the start in 1951 he joined *Drum*.

It was in 1952 that the fabulous character of Mr Drum was created. First the idea was a stunt whereby Mr Drum would disguise himself and walk through the locations. The first person who could identify him with a copy of *Drum* won a £5 note. Up to his death many people were still trying to earn a fiver off Henry.

But the idea of Mr Drum had too many tremendous possibilities. The first opportunity came with the famous Bethal story: farmers were rumoured to be ill-treating their labourers in the Bethal district and Henry was sent over to investigate as a labourer himself. He came back with a story that shook the whole country. 'Mr Drum Goes to Bethal' was the first Mr Drum exposure. And from there Henry had set *Drum* on the map.

Henry got himself arrested on the slight offence of not having a night pass and he went to jail. His experiences there made a chilling story that caused an international sensation. Now he regarded himself as a contemporary social historian.

Just about this time a friend of mine reading such stories in *Drum* said to me: 'This Mr Drum fellow is going bang into history ...'

Yes, so why the bloody hell did they have to choose him to murder? I cannot hide my bitterness at all. But, dear Henry, Mr Drum is not dead. Indeed, even while you lived, others were practising the game of Mr Drum. Now we shall take over where you left off. We want you, as you look down on us from among the angels, to mutter: 'The boys sure make a good job of that game, and looks like they might get the world a little cleaner from what I left it.'

Bye now.

Preface to *Darkness and Light*

This is us: Africa speaking to Africa and to the world. This anthology is not just about a grumpy, grousing South Africa, but about the whole of Africa: flamboyant West Africa, where men thrust elbows into each other's ribs and laugh broadly over their jokes; East Africa, with its strong Arab influence; traditional Africa, with the funny wisdom that lurks in the antics of animals and the ways of Ju-Ju men and witch doctors. Here are the dreams about the great things that we yet will do; the long dictionary words and the colourful regalia with which we swathe our dark bodies: that is us.

You can find us in the mealie fields and in the mines; you can find us in the shebeens quaffing 'Macbeth' brews to the jazz and jive of the cities, or outside the grass huts of our fathers, telling tales with the old women. You can see us gaffing each other or breaking suddenly into song and dance; into swear words, fighting and tears. We are here in the robes of our grandfathers and the tight-trousered dress of the big towns. All this is us.

Here, Africans are creating out of English a language of their own: a language that thinks in actions, using words that dart back and forth on quick-moving feet, virile, earthy, garrulous. Peggy Rutherfoord has delved deep into the literary store of our black Africa to compile this anthology, which shows us in the many moods that are ours. Somewhere or another on the continent there is a new civilisation beginning to appear, a new African culture – there are traces of it here.

CAN THEMBA

Drum Publications
15 Troye Street
Johannesburg
South Africa

Here it is at Last

Here it is at last – an anthology, collected from all over Africa, of the best writings by Africans that have appeared so far. And it comes – appropriately – from *Drum*. Jim Bailey, owner of *Drum*, commissioned Peggy Rutherfoord to gather the best of African writing into a single volume. She had to travel far and wide, she had to read and test and compare for four years before she felt she'd got together what she wanted.

Some of these stories, poems, verbal sketches were originally written in English, but many are translations of French, Portuguese and vernacular works. Almost every country in Africa is represented here.

Perhaps the growl is not here, but there is almost everything else. There are sweet, beautiful stories of young love and dances under the moon, the delightful pictures of a gleam upon the shimmering sea, the fantastic myths and legends of Africa. I didn't know these things still existed in Africa or that there were still men who contemplated them.

However, Africa is no more than just the vast playground. Events are moving so fast that even this admirable anthology inevitably misses many of the most significant trends and readers may be disappointed. Yet, in a very important sense, this book is part of the African Renaissance.

It has been said that a book of this nature was bound to be inadequate in the lack of a solid cultural background. But, surely, the point of the whole book is that it is its own background. It was brought to life in a society itself fast in transit, a society where the units were disparate before and now are solidifying. Perhaps I should be grateful that the book does not try to interpret contemporary Africa, as such. It tries to preserve what has been written, up to a given point.

But it is a pity that some of the latest, more vital and impatient writings by the people of Africa have not found a way into this anthology. I sadly miss the swift, quaint prose of Todd Matshikiza. The resigned humour of manhandled Casey Motsisi. The backyard strivings of Bloke Modisane, strivings to make Shakespeare and Bach still sound sweet in the noises and noisome odours of shebeen backyards.

It is not only in our political writing that the new, cheeky abuse of English has been applied so effectively. Of course, there will always be the pedants who will shudder at our barbarism. As they said about the African jazz opera, *King Kong*: 'Is this really culture?' Confound the culture ideas of those men! All we seek is the fullest expression of the bubbling life around us and the restless spirit within us.

Maybe this particular weakness in *Darkness and Light* is because Peggy Rutherfoord, who edited it, was a little too dazzled by the romantic Africa and failed to see – failed to feel – the hard reality of Africa. For the book fails to reflect convincingly the life of the urban African, his thoughts and reactions.

But who shall say what literature should be about? Much of the literature of protest has been trapped into sacrificing its sincerity for the cause. This does not detract from the justice and vitality of the cause. It does not even suggest that no great literature can come from great causes. But no artist will ever be content to substitute the noise of war for the music of *his* soul.

Spot Letter

I don't want to subvert the whole of our society – or what's left of it in these tattered times – but what must an honest minded man do when he finds that he has fallen genuinely in love with his neighbour's wife? I hate as much as the next man that sordid business of having an affair with another man's wife. I know all the overriding considerations of children involved, disruption of family life, the moral law. But I have seen too many pathetic alliances where husband and wife are dreadfully miserable because of one fatal mistake they had made in the headiness of youth. Must they be condemned to live together for ever? The snag become quite a noose when, say, the wife finds real love outside marriage. Petty moral replies of just 'Thou Shalt Not' do not assuage the agony. I'm not interested in the views of people with dirty minds, but I raise this matter in all seriousness because nowadays I've noticed many wives (and husbands) have secret affairs which I find strongly revolting. It happens in Dube, Orlando, all over the place. People tell me that George Goch actually holds the unholy record in this business. Surely, society should find a saner solution for these unhappy and frustrated people!

And just as surely grown men and women in this allegedly Broadminded Age will not be satisfied merely with condemnation. The clinical view, I suggest, should be based on freer and cheaper divorce, and not on free love.

Requiem for Sophiatown

Realism can be star-scattering, even if you have lived your whole unthinking life in reality. Especially in Sophiatown, these days, where it can come with the sudden crash of a flying brick on the back of your head.

Like the other day when Bob Gosani and I sneaked off towards our secret shebeen in Morris Street. We were dodging an old friend of ours whom we call the Leech, for he is one of those characters who like their drink – any amount – so long as someone else pays for it.

Well, this secret shebeen in Morris Street was a nice place. You take a passage through Meyer Street over haphazard heaps of bricks where houses have been broken down, you find another similar passage that leads you from Ray Street into Edith Street, where you find another passage, neater, having always been there, between the Coloured School and Jerusalem-like slum houses, you go down a little, and suddenly there it is.

Quite a fine place, too. A little brick wall, a minute garden of mostly Christmas flowers, a half-veranda (the other half has become a little kitchen) and the floor of the veranda polished a bright green.

Inside, the sitting room may be cluttered with furniture, it is so small, but you sink comfortably into a sofa as one of the little tables that can stand under the other's belly is placed before you, and you make your order. Half a jack of brandy!

How often have Bob and I not whooped happily: 'Yessus! The Leech will never find us here.' So, though there were directer routes to this place, we always took the passages. They say these people can smell when you are going to make a drink.

But that day, as we emerged into Morris Street, it was as if that brick had just struck us simultaneously on our heads. That sweet, little place was just not there. Where it should have been was a grotesque, grinning structure of torn red brick that made it look like the face of a mauled boxer trying to be sporting after his gruel. A nausea of despair rose up in me, but it was Bob who said the only appropriate thing: 'Shucks.'

Here is the odd thing about Sophiatown. I have long been inured to the ravages wreaked upon Sophiatown. I see its wrecks daily and, through many of its passages that have made such handy short cuts for me, I have stepped gingerly many times over the tricky rubble. Inside of me, I have long stopped arguing the injustice, the vindictiveness, the strong-arm authority of which prostrate Sophiatown is a loud symbol.

Long ago I decided to concede, to surrender to the argument that Sophiatown was a slum, after all. I am itchingly nagged by the thought that slum clearance should have nothing to do with the theft of freehold rights. But the sheer physical fact of Sophiatown's removal has intimidated me.

Moreover, so much has gone – veritable institutions. Fatty of the Thirty-nine Steps. Now, that was a great shebeen! It was in Good Street. You walked up a flight of steps, the structure looked dingy as if it would crash down with you any moment. You opened a door and walked into a dazzle of bright electric light, contemporary furniture and massive Fatty. She was a legend. Gay, friendly, coquettish, always ready to sell you a drink. And that mama had everything: whisky, brandy, gin, beer, wine – the lot. Sometimes she could even supply cigars. But now that house is flattened. I'm told that in Meadowlands she has lost the zest for the game. She has even tried to look for work in town. Ghastly.

Dwarf, who used to find a joke in everything. He used to walk into Bloke's place, catch us red-handed playing the music of Mozart. He used to cock his ear, listen a little and in his gravel voice comment: 'No wonder he's got a name like that.' There is nothing that Dwarf loved more than sticking out his tongue to a cop and running for it. I once caught him late at night in his Meadowlands house washing dishes. He still manfully tries to laugh at himself.

And Mabeni's, where the great Dolly Rathebe once sang the blues to me. I didn't ask her. She just sidled over to me on the couch and broke into song. It was delicious. But now Dolly is in Port Elizabeth, and Mabeni, God knows where.

These are only highlights from the swarming, cacophonous, strutting, brawling, vibrating life of the Sophiatown that was. But it was not all just shebeeny, smutty, illegal stuff. Some places it was as dreams are made on.

I am thinking of those St Cyprian's School boys who a decade ago sweatingly dug out the earth behind the house of the Community of the Resurrection, in order to have a swimming pool. It still stands, and the few kids left still paddle in it. Some of those early schoolboys of St Cyprian's later went up to Father Ross or Father Raynes or Father Huddleston who wangled a bursary for them to go to St Peter's, then on to Fort Hare, and later even Wits, to come back doctors.

Their parents, patiently waiting and working in town, skimped a penny here, a tickey there, so that they might make the necessary alteration to their house, or pay off the mortgage. And slowly Sophiatown was becoming house-proud.

Of course, there were pressures too heavy for them. After the war, many people came to Johannesburg to seek for work and some hole to night in. As they increased they became a housing problem. As nobody seemed to care, they made Sophiatown a slum.

But the children of those early Sophiatonians – some of them – are still around. It is amazing how many of them are products of the Anglican Mission at St Cyprian's. I meet them often in respectable homes and we talk the world to tatters.

Mostly we talk of our lot in life. After all, too often we have been told that we are the future leaders of our people. We are the young stalwarts who are supposed to solve the problems of our harassed world.

'Not political unity, we need,' one would say; 'our society is too diverse and unwieldy for that. Just a dynamic core of purified fighters with clear objectives and a straightforward plan of action. That is all.'

Another: 'No! We must align ourselves with the new forces at play in Africa today. There already is the dynamicity. The idea of a one Africa has never been put as powerfully as at Accra recently. You see, Africans, wherever they are, have not a territorial, a local loyalty: they don't feel that they belong to a South Africa or a Federation or a Tanganyika or a Kenya or a West Africa; but with Africans in the whole of Africa. In fact, many of us are wondering if Arabs and Egyptians are also Africans. They probably are.'

Still another: 'But if the boys in the North are getting busy, shouldn't we start something here ourselves?'

'Waal, you see, our ANC here has been caught with its pants down. The Africanists are claiming that Accra has proclaimed their stand. And the ANC representative there could only discuss the tactical difficulties of the ANC in South Africa with her special conditions.'

'Ya. But this African Personality idea, how does it mean to us? What does it mean, anyway?'

'I'll tell you. In the world today are poised against each other two massive ideologies: of the East and of the West. Both of them play international politics as if we're bound to choose between them. Between them only. We have just discovered that we can choose as we like, if we grow strong in our own character. But there's more to this. The West has had a damned long time to win us. Win us over to Western thinking. Western Christian way of living. Their ideas of democracy and their Christian ideals were wonderful, but they did not mean them.

'Let me explain. We are quite a religious people. We accept the idealism of Christianity. We accept its high principles. But in a stubborn, practical sense we believe in reality. Christian

Brotherhood must be real. Democracy must actually be the rule of the people: not of a white hobo over a black MA.

'To us, if a witch doctor says he'll bring rain, we not only want to see the rain fall, but also the crops sprout from the earth. That's what a rainmaker's for, nay? If the bone-thrower says he'll show up the bastard who's been slinging lightning at me, I expect him to swing that bolt of lightning right back. So if the priest says God's on my side, I'd like to see a few more chances and a little less whiteman's curses.

'But, in any case, Christianity is now an anaemic religion. It cannot rouse the ancient in me – especially the Shaka instinct I still have. Now, you and I are educated guys. We don't go for the witchcraft stuff. And we don't want to go for the jukebox stuff. But much as we deny it, we still want the thrill of the wild blood of our forefathers. The whites call it savagery. Ineradicable barbarism. But in different degrees we want the colour and vigour and vibrant appeal of it all. So the tsotsi seeks in the cowboy the way to strut across the streets with swaying hips and a dangerous weapon in each hand. So the Zionist thumps his drum and gyrates his holy fervour up the streets. So you and I and these guys here discuss politics, teasingly dancing around the idea of violence.

'All it means is that in wanting to express her demand for democratic self-determination, Africa is also releasing her ancientmost desire to live life over the brim. That's how come we sometimes seem to talk in two voices.'

'Wait a minute,' another shrieks, 'wait a minute. We're not all like that. Some of us would like to get things right and start anew. Some piece of social engineering could get things working right, if our moral purposes were right, not just vengeful.'

'Sure, but our masters have taught this damned thing violence so well by precept – often practice – that they get you to believe that it's the only way to talk turkey to them.'

We do not only talk about this particular subject. Our subjects are legion. Nkrumah must be a hell of a guy, or is he just bluffing? What about our African intellectuals who leave the country just when we need them most? But is it honestly true that we don't want to have affairs with white girls? What kind of white supremacy is this that cannot stand fair competition? What will happen if a real topmost Nat gets caught by the Immorality Act? In fact, all those cheeky questions that never get aired in public.

But it always ends up with someone saying, 'Aw shut up, folks, you got no plan to liberate us.'

Somewhere here, and among a thousand more individualistic things, is the magic of Sophiatown. It is different and itself. You don't just find your place here, you make it and you find yourself. There's a tang about it. You might now and then have to give way to others making their ways of life by methods not in the book. But you can't be bored. You have the right to listen to the latest jazz records at Ah Sing's over the road. You can walk a Coloured girl of an evening down to the Odin Cinema and no questions asked. You can try out Rhugubar's curry with your bare fingers without embarrassment. All this with no sense of heresy. Indeed, I've shown quite a few white people 'the little Paris of the Transvaal' – but only a few were Afrikaners.

What people have thought to be the brazenness of Sophiatown has really been its clean-faced frankness. And, of course, its swart jowl against the rosy cheek of Westdene.

Ay, me. That was the Sophiatown that was.

I shall have to leave these respectable homes of my friends and stumble over the loose bricks back to my den. I hear tell that Blackie is still about in his shack behind the posh house in devastated Millar Street.

Blackie's landlord is still facing it out, what the hell for? Since the Rathebe case most of the standholders have decided to capitulate. They are selling out like rats letting the passengers sink. Solly got caught in this – the newest racket. His landlord told him nothing. Waited for him to pay the next month's rent, although he knew that he was planning to sell out. The

Resettlement Board has been very sympathetic with such cases; it has told tenants not to pay landlords rent any more, for they may suddenly be given yesterday's notice and the GG will come to break down the house over their heads.

Solly was not at home when the landlord trekked. When he got there he found his furniture was left outside and a policeman was guarding the house. Poor Solly had to rush about looking for some place to put his stuff for the night. Half a dozen friends helped.

And still I wander among the ruins, trying to find one or two of the shebeens that Dr Verwoerd has overlooked. But I do not like the dead eyes with which some of these ghost houses stare back at me. One of these days I, too, will get me out of here. Finish and clear!

The Bottom of the Bottle

Comes a time when a man feels that everything in his personal organisation cannot much go on as before. No dramatic decision may be taken, in some bursting hour of change. But all the same, a man may feel that those in their bits of rag who have for so long been meekly begging at the gate of his mind, can no longer be joked or carefully drunk away.

I remember well one of those days during my bottle blindness in Sophiatown. We were in the House of Truth – my room at 111 Ray Street, Sophiatown, Johannesburg – I and all those young frustrated Africans who flitted through the half legal life of the urban African in the Union.

They were all there that day. Philip, the Health Inspector, who had been with me at Fort Hare; Peter, his younger brother, who was annually being baulked of Matriculation by the requirements of a supplementary examination in that malevolent subject, English (Higher Grade); Oubaas, the timeless one, who read morbid things like *The Inferno*, *Paradise Lost* and *Dr Faustus*; Maxie, scared still of two fingers of brandy, but obsessed with impressing the girls; the Kabaka (so called because his uncle once 'exiled' him from home for his shiftlessness); Jazzboy, miniature like the saxophone that brought him girls, liquor and an occasional beating up; I, their host.

The table was spired with bottles of brandy, gin, beer and we were at the stage of high discourse, much like the majestic demons in the burning pit.

For a moment, as I looked at those young men around me, the luxury of a mild flood of conscience swept over me. They had all at one time or another had visions: to escape their environment; to oppose and overcome their context; to evade and out-distance their destiny; by hard work and sacrifice, by education and native ability, by snatching from the table of occupation some of the chance crumbs of the high-chaired culture. Lord, it struck me, what a treasury of talent I have here in front of me. Must they bury their lives with mine like this under a load of Sophiatown bottles?

It was conscience that struck me, I say, because I knew that many of them looked up to me, my way of life, and repeated my despair and its defences behind my back. I knew that they were excited by me when I said: 'Why should one believe in anything, when one could live – live, gentlemen, at 212 degrees Fahrenheit? The trouble is, gentlemen, for me, human nature stinks; but that is all the material we have to work with.' They said these things I said. But never with my own deep sense of doubt, the sleepless, tossing suspicion that often made me itch in the very heat of my enthusiasm.

I think the rest of African society looked upon us as an excrescence. We were not the calm dignified Africans that the Church so admires (and fights for); not the unspoiled rural African the Government so admires, for they tell no lies, they do not steal and, above all, they do not try to measure up to the white man. Neither were we 'tsotsis' in the classical sense of the term, though the tsotsis saw us as cousins. I swear, however, that not one of the gentlemen who associated with me in that period was guilty (caught or not) of murder, rape, assault, robbery, theft or anything like that. True, we spent nights at police stations, but it was invariably for possession of illicit liquor or, its corollary, drunkenness. We were not 'cats', either, that sophisticated group of urban Africans who play jazz, live jazz and speak the township transmigrations of American slang.

We were those sensitive might-have-beens who had knocked on the door of white civilisation (at the highest levels that South Africa could offer) and had heard a gruff 'No' or a 'Yes' so shaky and insincere that we withdrew our snail horns at once.

An incident that Oubaas related to us illustrates this 'Yes'. He had been working for a white man of truly untraditional generosity of spirit. This boss allowed Oubaas to drive his car on private jaunts, to share lunch with him, to visit his house for a drink. Sometimes Oubaas even brought him into the nether world of the township where he liked the abandon of its denizens. And his politics? Positively anti-white, if not altogether subversive! They were back-slapping buddies, Oubaas and his boss.

Then one day there came into the shop – a chemist's – an old white lady. She gave her order and it turned into quite a fair-sized parcel. The old lady wanted to carry her parcel into her car, but the boss would have nothing of it. The old lady insisted that she could manage. And the boss insisted ...

'Don't worry, my *boy* will carry it out for you. That's what I hired the *native* for.'

Boy and *native* are hardly terms used in respectable race relations society. Something in the white man's intonation makes these innocuous words feel like barbed wire across a bare back.

Oubaas, normally not ungallant, was furious. But, for us, the joke was on Oubaas. He did not walk out on that nice boss at once, but went on working for him long months afterwards.

But for the most we savoured of life pungently. Living precariously, cheekily confronting the world's challenges. I, for myself, deliberately cocooned my mind away from the stirrings around it. 1948, the Nationalists took over power in South Africa. 1949, the Youth League forced their Programme of Action into African National Congress policy. 1952, the Defiance of Unjust Laws Campaign was launched. 1955, the massive Treason Arrests took place in predawn raids. 1960, Sharpeville! Colossal shadows of huge, angry politicians fell upon and affrighted us. Something there was that thundered in the skies.

Yet nightly we repaired to the House of Truth, swinging bottles of brandy filched from the dark cellars where the white man hid his courage from us, and drank ourselves cold.

By this time it was becoming clear to me that I was really fighting something inside that nibbled at my soaked soul. Yet, what the hell! We were cavaliers of the evanescent, romantics who turned the revolt inwards, upon our own bruised spirits. It was flight, now, no more just self-erasure.

Something happened one night that made me sit up and think. We had been drinking as usual and the casualties were lying all over my room: on the bed, over the studio couch, sprawled across the floor. I was sitting at the table, with a half full bottle in my hand, and trying to make a floosie who was too far out to distinguish Cupid from Dr Verwoerd. Then there came a knock on the door. I reeled over to open it and admit two very well-known politicians. The one was a shadow of a shadow, and he had that 'lean and hungry look'. But it was the other, bulkier man who really blurred through my half-consciousness.

He was huge and shaped like a barrel whose oblong began at the knees. He had arms like distorted zeppelins with Russian sausage fingers at their ends. His face ballooned at you as he breathed, and that face was black for you, wilfully black.

He spoke in a voice that was eternally hoarse.

'Can Themba, we'd like to talk to you,' he grated.

I motioned them into seats which they took like senators.

He wasted no time. 'Look,' he said, 'the fight is on. We know that you're not a membah, but this fight is for Ahfrich. We want you all, nice time boys' – here he looked at me accusingly – 'tsotsis, teachers, businessmen, lawyers, doctors, all! The Ahfrican Nahtional Congress is not a political party, it is the organisation of every Ahfrican, every Ahfrican.'

'But how do you know what I think?' I parried.

'Man,' came the lean man impatiently, 'you're black, are you not? You're an African, are you not? So long as you're black we know what you suffer and what you think.'

'I see,' I said evasively. 'What is it you want me to do?'

'We want your support, man,' said the big one, aghast at

this political moron. 'We hear that you've got some young men about you, and you can make them do things, do things that we don't think are in the nahtional interest. Will you be with us?'

I jerked up my thumb automatically and barked, 'Afrika!'

'Mayibuuuye!' they rasped.

They had risen at the salute and nearly upset the table. My bottle was staggering, but I caught it swiftly. I served a glass and offered them some, but they refused. I gulped my drink down so that the tears came to my eyes.

'So you are with us?' asked the big man as they prepared to go.

'Sure,' I said, 'sure,' hugging my beloved bottle.

But as they went out, I fancy I heard the lean one muttering: 'He's drunk, that's all.'

After that, perhaps largely because I paid more attention, I heard more and more *politics*: bitter, heady, virulent stuff. It expressed in venomous terms the wrath of a people who had come to the damn it all threshold. Also the despair of a people tied helplessly to an antheap: it was savage swearing. What struck me more those days was the great number of ordinary folk who spoke politics.

For the machine that was ploughing up the country could not leave one square inch undisrupted. In Zeerust, Sekhukhuneland, Pondoland, official policies were driving the tribesmen to resistance.

That was odd. Hitherto, the bad boys had been the urban Africans. They were 'spoiled', tried to 'imitate the white man', were the targets of 'agitators, Communists and tsotsis', and above all a sore to the segregationist faith of our masters by their insolent infiltration into the holy preserves of whitedom; they were the *black peril*, the direct descendants of the treacherous impis under Dingane, if you can take the contradiction.

But, increasingly now, our all tolerant country brothers rose up against the authorities, not in lawlessness, but because the Government's policy of retribalisation rode rough hooves over tribal custom and degraded the true position of the chief.

The tribal areas showed clearly that there had once been an ordered peaceful system by which tribes were able to live. It was a system of society and government that Africans knew to belong to their own customary sense of justice, and what was proper. The shadiest nuance of interpretation in the Kgotla (Tribal Council) could lead to spirited argument where even the chief could be required to explain his innovations. For the chief, too, was bound by custom.

With all its limitations, this other world composition served the needs of the times. It merged with the simple economy; it expressed the tribal psychology; slowly, with patient humour, it absorbed the wisdom and the philosophy of the fireplace – but it was so made that it could roar into violence at a moment's blowing.

The institutions of a system like this – a system that served the needs so well – could not just die, even with the change of times. They just adapted themselves by natural differentiation to new requirements. And the genuine among them asserted a new influence in an even more dynamic environment. The witch doctor's craft survives in the most revolutionary politics. The principle of *free debate* attends every discussion of significance. The women exert their oblique, but very effective influence on every project of importance.

But our old world tribal state was not to be left virgo intacta. The fifteenth century hurled at us the economic and adventurous recklessness of Europe and subsequently the mania called the 'Scramble for Africa' shuddered through the subcontinent. The sheer physical impact of the assault was enough to stagger the edifice of tribalism. I can almost see my infinitely great grandfather, leaping to his feet on a rock and gaping at a sailing ship seeking harbour – all his patriarchal dignity forgotten, as he exclaims, 'Hau!'

Yet these white men did not just bring things of wonder: the Floating House, the Booming Stick, the gaudy beads. They also brought ideas – evil, good, indifferent – ideas such as could subvert and demolish our tribal system. Funny, the idea with which they impressed us most is not Justice or Love Thy Neighbour or Liberty, Fraternity and Equality or Live and Let Live – no, but simply: you acquire a right to a right only by force. And they are still busy, through the centuries, trying to live down that spectacular bit of basic education. For us, it is only recently that you needed sugar-coated slogans to cover that profound 'truth' of Western, civilised morality.

But then we were barbarians both.

The ideas did their bit, but it was only when our labour was needed that a deliberate drive was made to haul us out of our tribal havens to come out to work. And where tribalism did not help to demonstrate 'the dignity of labour', tribalism had to be smashed. They were so bloody successful that now they fear they have drawn too many of us into the fields of urban industry and have sired themselves a problem.

Obsessed with the one purpose of smashing a tribal system that seemed to spurn the blandishments of the white economy and so frequently to defy white authority, the crusaders of Western Christian Civilisation sought not for a moment something in tribalism to be saved. The authority of the chiefs and of custom was scorned, the first called 'barbarian savages', and the second 'contrary to the principles of natural justice and civilisation'.

By Union the work of demolition was almost complete. All that remained now was the tidying of effective control over the Africans. It quickly became clear that the urban African was going to present the more intractable problem. He had so soon got the hang of the white man's ways. He did not turn a hair at slurs that his grasp of 'civilisation' was purely 'imitative', 'superficial', 'evanescent'. He just went on to learn how to drive a car, man a machine – good lord, he was even playing at trade unionism and politics!

Moreover, as the momentum of the initial process had not played itself out, more and more Africans were squeezed from the Reserves and the farms to try their luck in the cities. Again, they didn't give a damn for those who lamented 'the spoiling of the pure native', 'the falling for the temptation of cheap, city glitter', 'the misguidance of city spivs and incendiary agitators'. The city called and the peasants came.

Of course, some semblance of tribal integrity remained in the Reserves, but the migrant labour system made a pretty delinquent bastard out of it. Men came to the mines for a spell, lived in compounds and soured the city only in hectic excursions, then went back to awe their home-keeping brethren or to dismay their chiefs and elders with their outlandish ways.

But tribalism was crumbling all over and the Africans were fast becoming a race of city dwellers, with snatched visits to the Reserves. Hard economic and social laws dictated that these people would seek to adjust themselves into some form of permanence and security, and in the process demand the conditions that would facilitate such adjustment.

Somewhere near this point the authorities decided that the whole process of African urbanisation should be repudiated as a policy if not altogether as a fact, let the skies crack! And the simple method projected was the retribalisation of the people and the re-establishment of the authority of the chiefs – at least, that is, those chiefs who would keep their noses clean and obey the Government. And where tribal custom did not suit, for tribal custom chooses its own chiefs in its own way – well, who the hell is running the show, after all?

Meantime, however, other things had happened.

Largely because of the efforts of the African National Congress, but to as large an extent because of the industrial and population changes in the country and the excessive emphasis of white politics on *colour*, Africans were everywhere debunking tribalism and contemplating each other as *Africans*, themselves as a *nation* – whatever the guidebooks of the State Information Office say.

And this African view of themselves does not confine itself to South African blacks. It identifies itself with all the black people of Africa; it breathes out the 'African Personality'; it palpitates in time with the heartbeats of Accra. It strives hard to make itself vacuum enough to receive 'the winds of change' from the North. And against this there is nothing to engender a peculiar South African loyalty: not a black middle class; not a stake in the land, its wealth or, for that matter, its law, order and good government; nothing to make enough of them hesitate at the contemplation of this country's destruction.

The conflict between the opposed forces seems inevitable: the (roughly) white nationalism poised before the (not too roughly) black nationalism. The dilemma is so complete!

As I brood over these things, I, with my insouciant attitude to matters of weight, I feel a sickly despair which the most potent bottle of brandy cannot wash away. What can I do?

Crepuscule

The morning township train cruised into Park Station, Johannesburg, and came to a halt in the dark vaults of the subterranean platforms. Already the young of limb, and the lithe and lissom, had leapt off and dashed for the gate that would let them out. But the rest of us had to wade ponderously, in our hundreds, along the thickening platforms that gathered the populations disgorged by Naledi, Emdeni, Dube, Orlando, Pimville, Nancefield, Kliptown, Springs, Benoni, Germiston. Great maws that spewed their workership over Johannesburg.

I was in the press that trudged in the crowd on the platform. Slowly, good-humouredly we were forced, like the substance of a toothpaste tube, through the little corridor and up the escalator that hoisted us through the outlet into the little space of breath and the teeth of the pass-demanding South African Police.

But it was with a lilt in my step that I crossed the parquet foyer floor and slipped through the police net, because I knew which cop to pass by: the one who drank with me at Sis Julia's shebeen of an afternoon off. It was with a lilt, because it was spring as I walked out of Park Station into a pointillist morning with the sun slanting from somewhere over George Goch, and in spring the young ladies wear colourful frocks, glaring against the sunlight and flaring in the mischievous breezes. I joyed as I passed into Hoek Street, seeing the white girls coming up King George Street, the sunlight striking through their dresses, articulating the silhouettes beneath to show me leg and form; things black men are supposed to know nothing of and which the law asininely decrees may not even be imagined.

Funny thing this, the law in all its horrificiency prohibits me, and yet in the streets of Johannesburg I feast for free every morning. And, God, if I try hard enough, I may know for real in Hillbrow every night.

There is a law that says (I'm afraid quite a bit of this will seem like *there is a law that says*), well, it says I cannot make love to a white woman. It is law. But stronger still there is a custom – a tradition, it is called here – that shudders at the sheerest notion that any white man could contemplate, or any black man dare, a love affair across the colour line. They do: white men *do* meet and fall in love with black women; black men do explore 'ivory towers'. But all this is severely 'agin the law'.

There are also African nationalists who profess horror at the thought that any self-respecting black man could desire any white woman. They say that no African could ever so debase himself as to love a white woman. This is highly cultivated and pious lying in the teeth of daily slavering in town and in cinema. African girls, who are torturing themselves all the time to gain a whiter complexion, straighter hair and corset contained posteriors, surely know what their men secretly admire.

As for myself, I do not necessarily want to bed a white woman; I merely insist on my right to want her.

Once, I took a white girl to Sophiatown. She was a girl who liked to go with me and did not have the rumoured South African inhibitions. She did not even want the anthropological knowledge of 'how the other South Africans live'. She just wanted to be with me.

She had a car, an ancient Morris. On the way to Sophiatown of those days you drove along Bree Street, past the Fordsburg Police Station in the Indian area, past Braamfontein railway station, under the bridge away past the cemetery, past Bridgeman Memorial Hospital (known, strangely, for bringing illegitimate Non-European children into the world), up Hurst Hill, past Talitha Home (a place of detention for delinquent Non-European girls), past aggressive Westdene (sore at the proximity of so many Non-white townships around her), and into Sophiatown.

So that night a black man and a white woman went to Sophiatown. I first took Janet to my auntie's place in Victoria Road, just opposite the bus terminus. It was a sight to glad a cynic's heart to see my aunt shiver before Janet.

'Mama' – in my world all women equivalents of my mother are mother to me – 'Mama, this is my girl. Where is Tata?' This question, not because my uncle might or might not approve, but because I knew he was terribly fond of brandy, and I was just about to organise a little party; he would not forgive me for leaving him out. But he was not there. He had gone to some meeting of amagosa – church stewards, of whom he was the chief.

'Mama, how about a doek for Janet?'

The doek! God save our gracious doek. A doek is a colourful piece of cloth that the African woman wears as headgear. It is tied stylistically into various shapes from Accra to Cape Town. I do not know the history of this innocuous piece of cloth. In Afrikaans, the language of those of our white masters who are of Dutch and Huguenot descent, doek meant, variously, a tablecloth, a dirty rag or a symbol of the slave. Perhaps it was later used by African women in contact with European ideas of beauty who realised that 'they had no hair' and subconsciously hid their heads under the doek. Whatever else, the doek had come to designate the African woman. So that evening when I said, 'Mama, how about a doek for Janet', I was proposing to transform her, despite her colour and her deep blue eyes, into an African girl for the while.

Ma dug into her chest and produced a multicoloured chiffon doek. We stood before the wardrobe mirror while my sisters helped to tie Janet's doek in the current township style. To my sisters that night I was obviously a hell of a guy.

Then I took Janet to a shebeen in Gibson Street. I was well known in that particular shebeen, could get my liquor 'on tick' and could get VIP treatment even without the asset of Janet. With Janet, I was a sensation. Shebeens are noisy drinking places and as we approached that shebeen we could hear the blast of loud-mouthed conversation. But when we entered a haunted hush fell upon the house. The shebeen queen rushed two men off their chairs to make places for us, and: 'What would you have, Mr Themba?'

There are certain names that do not go with Mister, I don't have a clue why. But, for sure, you cannot imagine a Mr Charlie Chaplin or a Mr William Shakespeare or a Mr Jesus Christ. My name – Can Themba – operates in that sort of class. So you can see the kind of sensation we caused when the shebeen queen addressed me as Mr Themba.

I said, casually as you like, 'A half a jack for start, and I suppose you'd like a beer, too, my dear?'

The other patrons of the shebeen were coming up for air, one by one, and I could see that they were wondering about Janet. Some thought that she was Coloured, a South African Mulatto. One said she was white, appending, 'These journalist boys get the best girls.' But it was clear that the doek flummoxed them. Even iron-Coloureds, whose stubborn physical appearances veer strongly to the Negroid parent, are proud enough of whatever hair they have to expose it. But this girl wore a doek!

Then Janet spoke to me in that tinkling English voice of hers, and I spoke to her, easily, without inhibition, without madamising her. One chap, who could contain himself no longer, rose to shake my hand. He said, in the argot of the township, 'Brer Can, you've beaten caustic soda. Look, man, get me fish-meat like this, and s'true's God, I'll buy you a vung (a car)!' That sort of thawed the house and everybody broke into raucous laughter.

Later I collected a bottle of brandy and some ginger ale and took Janet to my room in Gold Street. There were a few friends and their girls: Kaffertjie (Little Kaffir – he was quite defiantly proud of this name) and Hilda, Jazzboy and Pule, Jimmy, Rockefeller and a Coloured girl we called Madame Defarge because, day or night, she always had clicking knitting needles with her. We drank, joked, conversed, sang and horseplayed. It was a night of the Sophiatown of my time, before the government destroyed it.

It was the best of times, it was the worst of times; it was the age of wisdom, it was the age of foolishness; it was the season of Light, it was the season of Darkness; it was the spring of hope, it was the winter of despair; we had everything before us, we had nothing before us; we were all going direct to Heaven, we were all going direct the other way – in short, the period was so far unlike the present period that some of its noisiest authorities insisted on its being received, for good or for evil, in the superlative degree of comparison only.

Sometimes I think, for his sense of contrast and his sharp awareness of the pungent flavours of life, only Charles Dickens – or, perhaps, Victor Hugo – could have understood Sophiatown. The government has razed Sophiatown to the ground, rebuilt it and resettled it with whites. And with appropriate cheek, they have called it Triomf.

That night I went to bed with Janet, chocolate upon cream. I do not know what happened to me in my sleep; the Africans say amadhlozi talked to me – the spirits of my forefathers that are supposed to guide my reckless way through this cruel life intervened for once. In the mid of the night I got up, shook Janet and told her we got to go.

'Ah, Can, you're disturbing me, I want to sleep.'

'Come-ahn, get up!'

'Please, Can, I want to sleep.'

I pulled off the blankets and marvelled awhile at the golden hair that billowed over her shoulders. Then she rose and dressed drowsily.

We got into her ancient Morris and drove to town. I think it was the remembrance of a half bottle of brandy in her room in Hillbrow that woke me and made me rouse her, more than the timely intervention of the amadhlozi. We saw a big, green kwela-kwela wire-netted lorry-van full of be-batonned white cops driving up Gold Street, but we thought little of it, for the cops, like fleas in our blankets, are always with us. So we spluttered up Hurst Hill into town.

Later I heard what had happened.

I used to have a young Xhosa girl called Baby. She was not really my class, but in those days for what we called love we Sophiatonians took the high, the middle and the low.

Baby was pathologically fond of parties, the type of parties to which tsotsis go. They organise themselves into a club of about half a dozen members. On pay day they each contribute, say, £5 and give it to the member whose turn it is. He then throws a party to entertain all the members and their girlfriends. Almost invariably guys trespass on other guys' girls and fights break out. Baby liked this kind of party, but it soon became clear to me that I was risking the swift knife in the dark so long as I associated with her. So I talked it over with her, told her that we should call it a day and that I did not want to clash with her tsotsi boyfriends. She readily accepted, saying, 'That-so it is, after all you're a teacher type and you don't suit me.'

So far as I was concerned that had been that.

But that star-crossed night Baby heard that I was involved with a white girl. She went berserk. I gathered that she went running down Gold Street tearing out her hair and shrieking. At the corner of Gold Street and Victoria Road, she met a group of tsotsis playing street football under the street lamp with a tennis ball. They asked her, 'Baby, whassamatter?' She screamed, 'It's Can, he's with a white woman,' and they replied, 'Report him!'

Africans are not on the side of the cops if they can help it. You do not go to a policeman for help or protection or the which way to go. You eschew them. To report a felon to them, good heavens! It is just not done. So for a tsotsi to say about anyone 'Report him!' means the matter is serious.

Baby went to Newlands Police Station and shouted, 'Baas, they're there. They're in bed, my boyfriend and a white woman.' The sergeant behind the counter told her to take it easy, to wait until the criminals were so well asleep that they might be caught flagrante delicto. But Baby was dancing with impatience at 'the law's delay'.

Still, that sergeant wanted to make a proper job of it. He organised a lorry full of white cops, white cops only, with batons and the right sadistic mental orientation. Or, perhaps, too many such excursions had misadventured before where black cops were suspected of having tipped off their brethren.

When we went down Gold Street, it was them we saw in the green lorry-van bent on a date with a kaffir who had the infernal impertinence to reach over the fence at forbidden fruit.

I understand they kicked open the door of my room and stormed in, only to find that the birds had flown. One white cop is reported to have said wistfully, 'Look, man, there are two dents in the pillow and I can still smell her perfume.' Another actually found a long thread of golden hair.

I met Baby a few days later and asked her resignedly, 'But you said we're no more in love, why the big jealous act?'

She replied, 'Even if we've split, you can't shame me for a white bitch.'

I countered, 'But if you still loved me enough to feel jealous, didn't you consider that you were sending me to six months in jail! Baby, it could be seven years, you know.'

'I don't care,' she said. 'But not with a white bitch, Can. And who says that I still love you? It's just that you can't humiliate me with a white bitch.'

I threw up my hands in despair and thought that one of these days I really must slaughter a spotlessly white goat as a sacrifice to the spirits of my forefathers. I have been neglecting my superstitions too dangerously long.

Funny, one of the things seldom said for superstitious belief is that it is a tremendous psychological peg to hang on to. God knows, the vehement attacks made upon the unreason and stark cruelty of superstition and witchcraft practices are warranted. Abler minds than mine have argued this. But I do want to say that those of us who have been detribalised

71

and caught in the characterless world of belonging nowhere have a bitter sense of loss. The culture that we have shed may not be particularly valuable in a content sense, but it was something that the psyche could attach itself to, and its absence is painfully felt in this white man's world where everything significant is forbidden, or 'Not for thee!' Not only the refusal to let us enter so many fields of human experience, but the sheer negation that our spirits should ever assume to themselves identity. Crushing.

It is a crepuscular, shadow life in which we wander as spectres seeking meaning for ourselves. And even the local, little legalities we invent are frowned upon. The whole atmosphere is charged with the white man's general disapproval, and where he does not have a law for it, he certainly has a grimace that cows you. This is the burden of the white man's crime against my personality that negatives all the brilliance of intellect and the genuine funds of goodwill so many individuals have. The whole bloody ethos still asphyxiates me. Ingratitude? Exaggeration? Childish, pampered desire for indulgence? Yes-yes, perhaps. But leave us some area in time and experience where we may be true to ourselves. It is so exhausting to have to be in reaction all the time. My race believes in the quick shaft of anger, or of love, or hate, or laughter: the perpetual emotional commitment is foreign to us. Life has contrived so much, such a variegated woof in its texture, that we feel we can tarry only a poignant moment with a little flare of emotion, if we are ever to savour the whole. Thus they call us fickle and disloyal. They have not yet called us hypocritical.

These things I claim for my race, I claim for all men. A little respite, brother, just a little respite from the huge responsibility of being a nice kaffir.

After that adventure in Sophiatown with Janet, I got a lot of sympathy and a lot of advice. I met the boys who had said to Baby, 'Report him!' I was sore because they had singled me out like that and made me the pariah that could be thrown to the wolves.

They put their case: 'You see, Brer Can, there's a man here on this corner who plays records of classical music, drinks funny wines and brings white men out here for our black girls. Frankly, we don't like it, because these white boys come out here for our girls, but when we meet them in town they treat us like turds. We don't like the way you guys play it with the whites. We're on Baby's side, Brer Can.'

'Look, boys,' I explained, 'you don't understand, you don't understand me. I agree with you that these whites take advantage of our girls and we don't like the way our girls act as if they are special. But all you've done about it is just to sit and sizzle here at them. No one among you has tried to take revenge. Only I have gone to get a white girl and avenged with her what the whites do to our sisters. I'm not like the guys who procure black girls for their white friends. I seek revenge. I get the white girls – well, it's tough and risky, but you guys, instead of sitting here crying your hearts out, you should get yourselves white girls, too, and hit back.'

I got them, I knew.

One guy said, 'By right, Brer Can's telling the truth.'

Another asked, 'Tell me, Brer Can, how does a white woman taste?'

That was going too far. I had too great a respect for Janet, the *woman*, to discuss that with anybody whether he was white or black.

I said, 'You go find out for yourself.'

The piece of advice I got from the mother of a friend of mine who stayed in the same street, Gold Street, was touching.

She said to me: 'Son, I've heard about your trouble with the white girl. It's you that was foolish. People know that your white girl is around because they recognise the car. If they see it parked flush in front of your house, they say, "Can has got silver-fish". What you should do is to drive the car into my yard here, right to the back of the house so that nobody could see it from the street, and then they wouldn't suspect that you have the white girl in your room down there.'

It seemed to me to be excellent, practical advice.

So the next time I got home with Janet we drove the car into the yard of my friend's mother, right back behind the house, and walked down in the dead of night to my room.

In the middle of the night my friend came clattering on the window of my room and shouted, 'Can, get up, the cops!' We got up, got dressed in breathless time, rushed to the car at his mother's place and zoomed out of Sophiatown on a little used route past St Joseph's Mission through Auckland Park into Hillbrow, where in the heart of the white man's flatland we could complete breaking the white man's law as, apparently, we could not do in Sophiatown.

Later I heard the sordid details of what had happened that night. My friend came home late and overheard his mother and sisters discussing the Morris we had left in their yard. The mother felt that it was not right that I should be messing around with a white woman when she had unmarried daughters of her own and my eligibility rated high. So she sent one of her daughters to go and tell Baby that I was with the white woman again and that I had left the car in their yard. My friend felt that he did not have the time to argue with his family, that his job was to warn us as quickly as he could to get the hell out of there.

As it turned out, I need not have bothered. The darling Afrikaner at the desk told Baby, 'Look here, woman, every time you have a quarrel with your boyfriend, you rush to us with a cock and bull story. Clear out!'

Kwashiorkor

'Here's another interesting case ...'

My sister flicked over the pages of the file of one of her case studies and I wondered what other shipwrecked human being had there been recorded, catalogued, statisticised and analysed. My sister is a social worker with the Social Welfare Department of the Non-European Section of the Municipality of Johannesburg. In other words, she probes into the derelict lives of the unfortunate poor in Johannesburg. She studies their living habits, their recreational habits, their sporting habits, their drinking habits, the incidence of crime, neglect, malnutrition, divorce, aberration, and she records all this in cyclostyled forms that ask the questions readymade. She has got so good that she could tell without looking whether such and such a query falls under paragraph so and so. She has got so clinical that no particular case rattles her, for she has met its like before and knows how and where to classify it.

Her only trouble was ferocious Alexandra Township, that hellhole in Johannesburg where it was never safe for a woman to walk the streets unchaperoned or to go from house to house asking testing questions. This is where I come in. Often I have to escort her on her rounds just so that no township roughneck molests her. We arranged it lovely so that she only went to Alexandra on Saturday afternoons when I was half day off and could tag along.

'Dave,' she said, 'here's another interesting case. I'm sure you would love to hear about it. It's Alex again. I'm interested in the psychological motivations and the statistical significance, but I think you'll get you a human interest story. I know you can't be objective, but do, I beg you, do take it all quietly and don't mess me up with your sentimental reactions. We'll meet at two o'clock on Saturday, okay?'

That is how we went to that battered house in Third Avenue, Alexandra. It was just a lot of wood and tin knocked together gawkily to make four rooms. The house stood precariously a few yards from the sour, cider-tasting gutter and in the back there was a row of out-rooms constructed like a train and let to smaller families or bachelor men and women. This was the main source of income for the Mabiletsa family – mother, daughter and daughter's daughter.

But let me refer to my sister Eileen's records to get my facts straight.

Mother: Mrs Sarah Mabiletsa, age 62, widow, husband Abner Mabiletsa died 1953 in motor car accident. Her sole sources of support are rent from out-rooms and working daughter, Maria. Sarah is dually illiterate.

Daughter: Maria Mabiletsa, age 17, Reference Book No F/V118/32N1682. Domestic servant. Educational standard: 5. Reads and writes English, Afrikaans, Sepedi. Convictions: 30 days for shoplifting. One illegitimate child unmaintained and of disputed paternity.

Child: Sekgametse Daphne Lorraine Mabiletsa, Maria's child, age 3 years. Father undetermined. Free clinic attendance. Medical report: Advanced Kwashiorkor.

Other relatives: Sarah's brother, Edgar Mokgomane, serving jail sentence, 15 years, murder and robbery.

Remarks (Eileen's verdict): This family is desperate. Mother: ineffectual care for child. Child: showing malnutrition effects. Overall quantitative and qualitative nutritional deficiency. Maria: good time girl, seldom at home, spends earnings mostly on self and parties. Recommend urgent welfare aid and/or intervention.

Although Eileen talks about these things clinically, *objectively*, she told me the story and I somehow got the feel of it.

Abner Mabiletsa was one of those people who was not content with life in the reserves in Pietersburg district where he was born and grew up. He did not see where the tribal set-up of chief and Kgotla – the tribal council – and customs, taboos, superstitions, witchcraft and the lackadaisical dreariness of rotating with the sun from morn till eve would take the people and would take him. Moreover, the urge to rise and go out to do things, to conquer and become someone, the impatience of the blood, seized him. So he upped and went to Johannesburg, where else? Everybody went there.

First, there were the ordinary problems of adjustment; the tribal boy had to fit himself into the vast, fast-moving, frenetic life in the big city. So many habits, beliefs, customs had to be fractured overnight. So many reactions that were sincere and instinctive were laughed at in the city. A man was continually changing himself, leaping like a flea from contingency to contingency. But Abner made it, though most of the time he did not know who he was, whither he was going. He only knew that this feverish life had to be lived, and identity became so large that a man sounded ridiculous for boasting he was a Mopedi or a Mosuto or a Xhosa or a Zulu – nobody seemed to care. You were just an African *here*, and somewhere *there* was a white man: two different types of humans that impinged, now and then – indeed often – but painfully.

Abner made it. He was helped by his home-boys, those who had come before. They showed him the ropes. They found him a job. They accommodated him those first few months until he found a room of his own in Alexandra. They took him to parties, to girls, to dice schools. Ultimately they showed him where he could learn to drive a car. Soon, soon, he could negotiate all the byways and back alleys of Johannesburg by himself. He had escapades, fun, riotous living … Until one day one of his escapades became pregnant and bore him a daughter. He paid the lobola – that hard dying custom of paying the bride price – getting some of his friends and home-boys to stand for him in loco parentis; he did not even apprise his folk back home in Pietersburg of his marriage; he did it all himself.

But life in Johannesburg was such that he did not find much time to look after his family. He was not exactly the delinquent father, but there was just not the time or the room for a man to become truly family bound. Then suddenly, crash! He died in a motor car accident and his unprovided for wife had to make do.

His daughter, Maria, grew up in the streets of Alexandra. The spectre of poverty was always looming over her life; and at the age of fourteen she left school to work in the white man's kitchens. It helped, at first, to alleviate the grim want, the ever empty larder at home. But soon she got caught up in the froth of Johannesburg's titillating nether life. She had a boyfriend who came pretty regularly to sleep in her room at the back of her place of employment; she had other boyfriends in the city, in the townships, with whom she often slept. And of the billions of human seed so recklessly strewn, one was bound some time to strike target.

When her condition became obvious, Maria nominated the boy she liked best, the swankiest, handsomest, most romantic and most moneyed swain in her repertoire. But he was a dangerous tsotsi, and when she told him of what he had wrought, he threatened to beat the living spit out of her. She fondly, foolishly persisted; and he assaulted her savagely. The real boyfriend – the one who slept in her room – felt bitter that she had indicated another. Had he not already boasted to his friends that he had 'bumped' her? Now the whole world judged that he had been cuckolded.

Poor Maria tried the somersault and turned to him, but by then he would have none of it. He effectively told the Native Commissioner, 'I am this girl's second opinion. She does not know who is responsible for her condition. There she stands, now too scared to nominate the man she first fancied, so she looks for a scapegoat, me.'

The commissioner had some biting things to say to Maria and concluded that he could not, in all conscience, find this man guilty of her seduction. As they say, he threw out the case.

So Sekgametse Daphne Lorraine was born without a father;

an event in Alexandra, in Johannesburg, in all the urban areas of our times, that excites no surprise whatsoever.

First, Maria shed all her love – that is, the anguish and pain she suffered, the bitterness, the humiliation, the sense of desolation and collapse of her tinsel world – upon this infant. But people either perish or recover from wounds; even the worst afflictions do not gnaw at you forever. She went back to her domestic work, leaving the baby with her mother. She would come home every Thursday – Sheila's Day – or the day off for all the domestics in Johannesburg. She came to her baby, bringing clothing, blankets, pampering little goodies and smothering treacly love.

But she was young still and the blood burst inside her once she recovered. Johannesburg was outside there calling, calling, first wooingly, alluringly, then more and more stridently, irresistibly. She came home less often, but remorsefully, and would crush the child to her in those brief moments. Even as she hugged the rose, the thorns tore at her. Then suddenly she came home no more ...

'It is quite a typical case of recidivism,' Eileen explained scholastically to me on our way to Alexandra. 'You see, there's a moment's panic as a result of the trauma. The reaction varies according to the victim. One way is that for most of our girls there's a stubborn residue of moral upbringing from home or school or church, sometimes really only from mamma's personality, and mamma probably comes from an older, steadier, more inhibited and tribe-controlled environment ...' Eileen shrugged helplessly, '... and detribalisation, modernisation, adaptation, acculturation, call it what you like, has to tear its way into their psychological pattern, brute-like. At first, before the shock, these girls really just float loosely about in the new freedoms, not really willing evil, not consciously flouting the order, but they're nevertheless playing with fire, and there's no one knows to tell them no. Their parents themselves are baffled by what the world's come to and there's no invisible reality like tribe, or comprehensible code like custom or taboo, to keep some kind of balance. Meanwhile the new dispensation – the superior culture, they call it; the diabolical shadow life, I call it – pounds at them relentlessly. Suddenly some traumatic event, a jail sentence, a sudden encounter with brute, bloody death, or a first pregnancy, pulverises them into what we credulous monitors consider repentance. It's really the startled whimper of a frightened child vaguely remembering that in some remote distance mamma or tribe or school or church has whispered, "Thou shalt not," and the horror that it's too late.

'But,' Eileen almost cursed out the words, 'the superior culture keeps pounding at them, and it's a matter of time before your repentant maiden sings again, "Jo'burg, here I come".'

I was shaken. 'Eileen, you know that much and yet you consider tinkling with statistics!'

She pulled herself together with an effort. But though she spoke confidently, it sounded unconvincing: 'Lad, I'm a social scientist, not a conjuress.'

So we went to that house in Third Avenue, off Selbourne Street. A deep gully ran in front of the house but the uneven street did not allow it to function effectively as a drain, and puddles of murky, noisome water and collected waste matter stood pooled in it, still, thick, appalling, like foul soup that makes you nauseous – as if some malevolent devil bade you gulp it down. On the other side the rotting carcass of a long dead dog was sending malodorous miasmata from its surface to befoul the air. And on either side the street, moated by these stinking gullies, lived people.

Eileen jumped smartly over the trench and I followed. We walked into the fenceless yard, round to the back of the house, and she knocked. After a moment a wrinkled old lady opened the door. The ploughshares of the years had wobbled across her face; but then again, you thought it could not have been the years alone that had ravaged her so; something else ...

'Oh, come in, nurse.' They called everybody 'nurse' who came to their hovels to promise assuagement of their misery.

Although it was bright day outside, you had to get used to the dark inside, and then when your eyes, by slow degrees, adjusted themselves, things seemed to come at you. A big sideboard tilted into view first. Then a huge stove whose one grey arm reached into the ceiling hole obscenely, and near it a double-bed, perched on four large polish tins filled with sand. The bed was sunken in the middle like a crude canoe and the blankets on it were yellow with age and threadbare with wear. In the middle of the top blanket was a great hole from some past misadventure and through the hole glowered a crimson eye, the red disc of a piece-patched quilt-like thing.

I stumbled into a wooden table in the centre and in my retreat hit a kitchen dresser. Dark brown cockroaches scrambled for cover.

'Don't be so clumsy,' Eileen hissed, and in the same syntax, as it were, to the old lady, 'Mother Mabiletsa, it's so dark in here. You really must open that window.'

I had not known there was a window there, but Eileen swept a piece of blanket aside and in flushed the light of day.

'How are you, Mother Mabiletsa? How are the legs today? Sit down please and tell me how is the baby.'

Mother Mabiletsa groaned into a chair and I took a bench by the side of the table. Eileen stood a moment, holding the old woman in scrutiny. When the old woman did not reply, Eileen lifted her bag and put it on the table.

'Look, I've brought little Sekgametse some skimmed milk. It's very good for babies, you know.'

I turned to look at the old lady and it seemed to me she was past caring about either Grace or Damnation. She was just enveloped in a dreadful murk of weariness.

She pressed down on arthritic knees, rose painfully and limped into another room. I could hear her moving about, heaving with effort though she sounded alone. Then she came in with a bundle in her arms which she put down on the great bed beside Eileen.

'Come and look,' Eileen whispered to me as she unfurled

the bundle.

There sat a little monkey on the bed. It was a two to three years' old child. The child did not cry or fidget, but bore an unutterably miserable expression on its face, in its whole bearing. It was as if she was the grandmother writ small; pathetically, wretchedly she looked out upon the world.

'Is it in pain?' I asked in an anxious whisper.

'No, just wasting away.'

'But she looks quite fat.'

To be sure, she did. But it was a ghastly kind of fatness, the fatness of the 'hidden hunger' I was to know. The belly was distended and sagged towards the bed. The legs looked bent convexly and there were light brown patches on them, and on the chest and back. The complexion of the skin was unnaturally light here and there so that the creature looked piebald. The normally curly hair had a rusty tint and had lost much of its whorl. Much of it had fallen out, leaving islets of skull surfacing.

The child looked aside towards me and the silent reproach, the quiet, listless, abject despair flowed from the large eyes wave upon wave. Not a peep, not a murmur. The child made no sound of complaint except the struggling breathing.

But those haunted eyes of despair. Despair? I brooded. To despair, you should have had knowledge before. You should have gone through the tart sensations of experience, have felt the first flush of knowledge, the first stabs of hope, have encountered reality and toyed with the shifting, tantalising promises that shadow play across life's tapestries, have stretched out, first tentative arms, then wildly grasping hands, and have discovered the disappointment of the evanescence of all things that come from the voids to tickle men's fancies, sharpen men's appetites and rouse their futile aspirations, only to vanish back into the voids. Ultimately you should have looked into the face of death and known the paralysing power of fear.

What of all this, could this little monkey know? And yet

there it all was in those tragic eyes.

Then I thought, 'So this is *kwashiorkor!*' Hitherto, to me, the name had just been another scare-word that had climbed from the dark caves of medical nomenclature to rear its head among decent folk; it had been another disgusting digit, a clipped statistic that health officials hurled at us reporters, and which we laced our copy with to impress sensation seeking editors who would fulminate under headlines like KWASHIORKOR AT YOUR DOOR. It had seemed right, then almost sufficient that we should link it with the other horrors like 'Infant Mortality', 'Living Below the Breadline', 'The Apathy of the People' and 'The Cynical Indifference of the Affluent Society to the Problem'.

But here in this groanless, gloomy room, it seemed indecent to shriek banner headlines when the child, itself, was quiet. It spoke no protest, it offered no resistance.

But while I was romanticising, my sister was explaining to the old lady how to care for and feed the child, how to prepare and use the skim milk, how often to give it Cod Liver Oil, how often to take it out into the air and the sunlight, how often to take it to the clinic.

Her mistressy voice, now urgent and straining, now clucking and scolding, now anxiously explaining, thinking in English, translating to itself first into Sepedi, begging, stressing, arguing, repeating, repeating, repeating – that restless voice tinkled into my consciousness, bringing me back.

The old lady muttered, 'I hear you, child, but how can I buy all these things with the R1.50 that's left over each month, and how can I carry this child to the clinic with my creaking bones?'

I was subdued.

'Well,' said Eileen later as we returned to the bus stop. 'Think you've seen bottomless tragedy? I could give you figures for kwashiorkor in Alexandra alone ...'

'Please, Eileen, please.'

My life, a reporter's life, is rather full and hectic, and I am so vortically cast about in the whirlpools of Johannesburg that no single thought, no single experience, however profound, can stay with me for long. A week, two weeks, or less, and the picture of the kwashiorkor baby was jarred out of me, or perhaps lost into the limbo where the psyche hides unpleasant dreams.

Every day during that spell I had to traffic with the ungodly, the wicked, the unfortunate, the adventurous, the desperate, the outcast and the screwy.

One day, I was in E Court waiting for a rather spectacular theft case to come. I had to sit through the normal run of petty cases. I was bored and fishing inside myself for a worthwhile reverie when suddenly I heard: 'Maria Mabiletsa! Maria Mabiletsa!' My presence of mind hurried back.

The prosecutor said, 'This one is charged with receiving stolen goods, Your Worship.'

A white man rose and told the court, 'Your Worship, I appear for the accused. I M Karotsky, of Mendelsohn and Jacobs, Sans Souci House, 235 Bree Street.'

The prosecutor asked for an adjournment as 'other members of the gang are still at large'.

There was a wrangle about bail, but it was refused and the case was adjourned to August 25th.

It jolted me. After my case I went down to the cells, and there, after sundry buffetings despite the flashing of my Press Card, I managed to see her.

She was sweet; I mean, looked sweet. Of course, now she was a mixture of fear and defiance, but I could see beyond these facades the real simplicity of her.

I do not know how long she had been in the cells, but she was clean and looked groomed. Her hair was stretched back and neatly tied in the ring behind the crown. She had an oval face, eyes intelligent and alive. Her nose stood out with tender nostrils. Her mouth was delicate but now twisted into a bitter scowl and a slender neck held her head like the stem of a flower. Her skin colour was chestnut, but like ... like ...

like the inside of my hand. She had a slight figure with pouts for breasts, slight hips, but buttocks rounded enough to insist she was African. She wore atop a white blouse with frills, and amidships one of those skirts cut like a kilt, hugging her figure intimately and suddenly relenting to flare out.

But now she was importunate. For her all time was little and lots had to be said quickly. Before I could talk to her she said, 'Au-boetie, please, my brother, please, go and tell Lefty I'm arrested. Marshall Square maybe No 4. Tell him to bail me out. I'm Maria Mabiletsa, but Lefty calls me Marix. Please, Au-boetie, please.'

'Easy Maria,' I soothed, 'I know about you. I'm Dave from *The Courier*.'

'Hô-man, Boeta Dave, man. You we know, man. I read *The Courier*. But, please, Boeta Dave, tell Lefty my troubles, my mother's child.'

A cop was hurrying them away. 'Come'n, phansi – down! Phansi! – down!'

'Please, Au-boetie Dave, don't forget to tell Lefty!'

'Maria,' I shouted as she was being rushed off, 'I've seen Sekgametse, she's well looked after.'

'Oh! – '

'Phansi – down!' Bang! The iron gates fell with a clangour.

That night I told Eileen. She stared at me with knitted brows for a long time. Then she said, 'The main thing is not to panic the old lady. Saturday, you and I will have to go there, but don't do or say anything to make her panic. Leave me to do all the talking.' But I could see Eileen was near panic herself.

Then I went to see Lefty. He was suave, unperturbed, taking all this philosophically.

'You reporter boys take everything to head. Relax. You must have rhythm and timing. I've already got Karotsky to look after her and tomorrow Marix will be out. Relax, and have a drink.'

She was not out that tomorrow nor the day after. She had to wait for August 25. Meantime, Saturday came and Eileen and I went to the house in Third Avenue, Alexandra. When we got there we found – as they say – 'House To Let'. The old lady had heard about what had happened to Maria; she was faced with debts and the threat of starvation, so she packed her things, took the child and returned to the reserve in Pietersburg.

The neighbours shrugged their shoulders and said, 'What could the old lady do?'

Eileen was livid.

'Dave, do you know what this means?' she erupted. 'It means that child is doomed. In the country, they love children, they look after them, they bring them up according to a code and according to what they *know*, but what they know about the nutrition of children is homicidal and, s'true's God, they live under such conditions of poverty that they may turn cannibals any moment. That's where goes the child I tried to rehabilitate. And when adversity strikes them, when drought comes and the land yields less and less, and the cows' udders dry up, who are the first to go without? The children, those who need the milk most, those who need the proteins, the fats, the oils, the vegetables, the fruit; of the little there is, those who need it most will be the first to go without. A doctor once told me, Dave, "Kwashiorkor hits hardest between the ages of one and five when protein is needed most and when it's least available to African children." Least available! Why, Dave, why? Because the ignorant African does not realise that when milk is short, give the children first; when meat is little, give the children first. It's not as if ...' she wailed '... it's not as if my over-detribalised self wants to give grown-ups' food to children, but my Sekgametse's sick. I've been trying to coax her back from unnecessary and stupid child death. Now this.'

Tactlessly, I said, 'Come now, Eileen, you've done your bit. Go and make your report; you're not a nurse, and in any case you can't solve the whole world's troubles one out.'

'The whole world's troubles!' she spat at me as if I was a child stealer. 'I only wanted to save that one child, damn you!'

Of course, she made her social worker's report, and other

human problems seized her, and I often wondered later whether she had forgotten her kwashiorkor baby. Once, when I asked her if she had heard anything about the baby, she gave a barbed-wire reply, 'Outside our jurisdiction.' It sounded too official to be like Eileen, but I sensed that she felt too raw about it to be anything else than professional, and I held my war within me.

Then I met Maria. It was at a party in Dube, one of those class affairs where thugs and tarts appear in formal dress, and though none of the chicken flew, the liquor flowed.

'Remember me?' I asked her in the provocative style in vogue.

She screwed her face and wrinkled her nose and said, 'Don't tell me, don't tell me, I know I know you.' But strain as hard as she tried, she could not identify me. So in mercy I told her I was the news reporter she once sent to Lefty when she was arrested. It half registered. I told her my sister was the 'nurse' who looked after her Sekgametse. A cloud crossed her brow.

'Hê, man, Au-boetie, man, Africans are cruel,' she moaned. 'You know, I sent my child to the reserve in Pietersburg, and every month I used to send her nice things until she was the smartest kid in the countryside. Then they bewitched her. *Kaffir poison!*' she said darkly. 'The child's stomach swelled and swelled with the beast they'd planted in it, until the child died. The Lord God will see those people, mmcwi!'

Viciously I asked: 'And did you ever send the child soya beans?'

The Will to Die

I have heard much, have read much more, of the Will to Live; stories of fantastic retreats from the brink of death at moments when all hope was lost. To the aid of certain personalities in the bleakest crises, spiritual resources seem to come forward from what? Character? Spirit? Soul? Or the Great Reprieve of a Spiritual Clemency – hoisting them back from the muddy slough of the Valley of the Shadow.

But the Will to Die has intrigued me more ...

I have also heard that certain snakes can hypnotise their victim, a rat, a frog or a rabbit, not only so that it cannot flee to safety in the overwhelming urge for survival, but so that it is even attracted towards its destroyer and appears to enjoy dancing towards its doom. I have often wondered if there is not some mesmeric power that Fate employs to engage some men deliberately, with macabre relishment, to seek their destruction and to plunge into it.

Take Foxy ...

His real name was Philip Matauoane, but for some reason, I think from the excesses of his college days, everybody called him Foxy. He was a teacher in a small school in Barberton, South Africa. He had been to Fort Hare University College in the Cape Province and had majored in English (with distinction) and Native Administration. Then he took the University Education Diploma (teaching) with Rhodes University, Grahamstown.

He used to say, 'I'm the living exemplar of the modern, educated African's dilemma. I read English and trained to be a teacher – the standard profession for my class those days; but you never know which government department is going to expel you and pitchfork you into which other government department. So I also took Native Administration as a safety device.'

You would think that that labels the cautious, providential kind of human.

Foxy was a short fellow, the type that seems in youth to rush forward towards old age, but somewhere around the eve of middle age stops dead and ages no further almost forever. He had wide, owlish eyes and a trick with his mouth that suggested withering contempt for all creation. He invariably wore clothes that swallowed him: the coat overflowed and drowned his arms, the trousers sat on his chest in front and billowed obscenely behind. He was a runt of a man.

But in that unlikely body resided a live, restless brain.

When Foxy first left college, he went to teach English at Barberton High School. He was twenty-five then, and those were the days when high school pupils were just ripe to provoke or prejudice a young man of indifferent morals. He fell in love with a young girl, Betty Kumalo, his own pupil.

I must explain this spurious phenomenon of 'falling in love'. Neither Foxy nor Betty had the remotest sense of commitment to the irrelevance of marrying some day. The society of the times was such that affairs of this nature occurred easily. Parents did not mind much. Often they would invite a young teacher to the home, and as soon as he arrived would eclipse themselves, leaving the daughter with stern but unmistakable injunctions to 'be hospitable to the teacher'.

We tried to tell Foxy, we his fellow teachers, that this arrangement was too nice to be safe, but these things had been written in the stars.

Foxy could not keep away from Betty's home. He could not be discreet. He went there every day, every unblessed day. He took her out during weekends and they vanished into the countryside in his ancient Chevrolet.

On Mondays he would often say to me, 'I don't know what's wrong with me. I know this game is dangerous. I know Betty will destroy me, but that seems to give tang to the adventure. Hopeless. Hopeless,' and he would throw his arms out.

I had it out with him once.

'Foxy,' I said, 'you must stop this nonsense. It'll ruin you.'

There came a glint of pleasure, real ecstasy it seemed to me, into his eyes. It was as if the prospect of ruin was hallelujah.

He said to me, 'My intelligence tells me that it'll ruin me, but there's a magnetic force that draws me to that girl, and another part of me, much stronger than intelligence, just simply exults.'

'Marry her, then, and get done with it.'

'No!' He said it so vehemently that I was quite alarmed. 'Something in me wants that girl pregnant but not a wife.'

I thought it was a hysterical utterance.

You cannot go flinging wild oats all over a fertile field, not even wild weeds. It had to happen.

If you are a schoolteacher, you can only get out of a situation like that if you marry the girl, that is if you value your job. Foxy promptly married – another girl! But he was smart enough to give Betty's parents £50. That, in the hideous system of lobola, the system of bride price, made Betty his second wife. And no authority on earth could accuse him of seduction.

But when his wife found out about it, she battered him, as the Americans would say, 'To hell and back'.

Foxy started drinking heavily.

Then another thing began to happen; Foxy got drunk during working hours. Hitherto, he had been meticulous about not cultivating one's iniquities in the teeth of one's job, but now he seemed to be splashing in the gutter with a will.

I will never forget the morning another teacher and I found him stinkingly drunk about half an hour before school was to start. We forced him into a shebeen and asked the queen to let him sleep it off. We promised to make the appropriate excuses to the headmaster on his behalf. Imagine our consternation when he came reeling into the assembly hall where we were saying morning prayers with all the staff and pupils. How I prayed that morning!

These things happen. Everybody noticed Foxy's condition

except, for some reason, the headmaster. We hid him in the Biology Laboratory for the better part of the day, but that did not make the whole business any more edifying. Happily, he made his appearance before we could perjure ourselves to the headmaster. Later, however, we learned that he had told the shebeen queen that he would go to school perforce because we other teachers were trying to get him into trouble for absence from work and that we wished to 'outshine' him. Were we livid?

Every one of his colleagues gave him a dressing-down. We told him that no more was he alone in this: it involved the dignity of us all. The whole location was beginning to talk nastily about us. Moreover, there was a violent, alcoholic concoction brewed in the location called Barberton. People just linked 'Barberton', 'High' and 'School' to make puns about us.

Superficially it hurt him to cause us so much trouble, but something deep down in him did not allow him really to care. He went on drinking hard. His health was beginning to crack under it. Now, he met every problem with the gurgling answer of the bottle.

One night I heard that he was very ill, so I went to see him at home. His wife had long since given him up for lost; they no more even shared a bedroom. I found him in his room. The scene was ghastly. He was lying in his underwear in bed linen which was stained with the blotches of murdered bugs. There was a plate of uneaten food that must have come the day before yesterday. He was breathing heavily. Now and then he tried to retch, but nothing came up. His bloodshot eyes rolled this way and that, and whenever some respite graciously came, he reached out for a bottle of gin and gulped at it until the fierce liquid poured over his stubbled chin.

He gibbered so that I thought he was going mad. Then he would retch violently again, that jolting, vomitless quake of a retch.

He needed a doctor but he would not have one. His wife carped, 'Leave the pig to perish.'

I went to fetch the doctor nevertheless. We took quite a while, and when we returned, his wife sneered at us, 'You wouldn't like to see him now.' We went into his room and found him lost in oblivion. A strange girl was lying by his side.

In his own house!

I did not see him for weeks, but I heard enough. They said that he was frequenting dangerous haunts. One drunken night he was beaten up and robbed. Another night he returned home stark naked, without a clue as to who had stripped him.

Liquor should have killed him, but some compulsive urge chose differently. After a binge one night, he wandered hopelessly about the darksome location streets, seeking his home. At last, he decided on a gate, a house, a door. He was sure that that was his home. He banged his way in, ignored the four or five men singing hymns in the sitting room and staggered into the bedroom. He flung himself on to the bed and hollered, 'Woman, it's time that I sleep in your bed. I'm sick and tired of being a widower with a live wife.'

The men took up sticks and battered Foxy to a pulp. They got it into their heads that the woman of the house had been in the business all the time; that only now had her lover gone and got drunk enough to let the cat out of the bag. They beat the woman, too, within millimetres of her life. All of them landed in jail for long stretches.

But I keep having a stupid feeling that somehow, Philip 'Foxy' Matauoane would have felt: 'This is as it should be.'

Some folks live the obsession of death.

Ten to Ten

The curfew proper for all Africans in Marabastad, Pretoria, was 10 pm. By that hour every African, man, woman and child, had to be indoors, preferably in bed; if the police caught you abroad without a 'special permit' you were hauled off to the battleship-grey little police station in First Avenue, near the Aapies River, and clapped in jail. The following morning you found yourself trembling before a magistrate in one of those out-rooms that served as a court, and after a scathing lecture you were fined ten bob. So it behove everyone, every black mother's son, to heed that bell and be off the streets at ten.

But it was strange how the first warning bell at ten to ten exercised a power of panic among us, really out of all proportion. I suppose, watchless at night, when that bell went off and you were still streets away from your house, you did not know whether it was the first warning – ten to ten – giving you that much grace to hurry you on, or the fatal ten o'clock bell itself.

However, there were ever women in their yards, peering over corrugated iron fences and bedstead gates calling in sing-song voices, 'Ten to ten! Ten to ten!' as if the sound of the bell at the police station down there in First Avenue was itself echoed, street after street, urging the belated on, homewards, bedwards, safe from the Law.

As the first bell rang, one Saturday night, a huge African policeman roused himself from the barracks. He was enormous. Nearer seven feet than six feet tall, he towered over his fellow men like a sheer mountain above the mites in the valley. Perfectly formed, his shoulders were like boulders, his arms like the trunks of elephants, the muscles hard and corded. His legs bore his magnificent torso like sturdy pillars under some granite superstructure. He had the largest foot in Pretoria, size 15, and people used to say, 'His boot is special made from the factory'. He was coal-black, with the shiny blackness of ebony, but had large, rolling, white eyes and thick, bluish lips.

He gave a last, critical scrutiny to his shining, black boots and black uniform with tinny buttons, before he stepped into the charge office to report for duty. His was the night beat. Every night at ten o'clock he went out with one or two other policemen to roam the slummy streets of Marabastad Location and clear them of vagrants. People looked at him with awe; nobody ever argued with him; when his immense shadow fell across you, you shrivelled or, if you had any locomotion left in you, you gave way fast.

They called him Ten to Ten because of that night beat of his and he was known by no other name. Ten to Ten's strength was prodigious and there were many legends in the location about him ...

There was the one that he originally came from Tzaneen in Northern Transvaal to seek work in Pretoria. One day he was sitting in a drinking house when a young location hooligan came in and molested the daughter of the house. The girl's father tried to protest but the young hooligan slapped him across the face and told him to shut up. Ten to Ten was not accustomed to such behaviour, so he rose from the corner where he was sitting with his tin of beer and walked up to the young man.

'Look,' he said 'you can't go on like this in another man's house. Please go away now.' He gently pushed the young man towards the door. 'Come on, now, go home.'

The young man swung round with a curse, hesitated a moment as he saw the great bulk of the man confronting him, then with a sneer drew a knife.

They say you can pester a Venda from the North, you can insult him, you can humiliate him in public or cheat him in private, but there are two things you just cannot do with impunity: take his girl or draw a knife on him.

That night, Ten to Ten went jungle-mad.

'Ha!' he snarled.

The knife flashed and caught him in the forearm, blood spurting. But before the young man could withdraw it, Ten to Ten had caught him by the neck and dragged him out of the house. In the yard there was the usual corrugated iron fence. Swinging the boy like wet laundry, Ten to Ten lashed him at the fence repeatedly until the fence broke down. Then he started strangling him. Men came running out of the houses. They tried to tear Ten to Ten off the boy, but he shook them off like flakes. Soon, somebody sounded a whistle, the call for the police. By the time they came Ten to Ten was wielding and hurling all sorts of at hand weapons at the small crowd that sought to protect the boy.

The police stormed him and knocked him over, bludgeoning him with batons. They managed to manacle his wrists while he was down on his back, then they stepped back wiping the sweat off and waiting for him to rise. Ten to Ten rose slowly on one knee. He looked at the police and smiled. The white sergeant was still saying, 'Now, now, come quietly, no more trouble, eh?' when Ten to Ten spotted his enemy staggering from the crowd.

He made a savage grunt and, looking at his bound hands, he wrenched them apart and snapped the iron manacles like cotton twine. The police had to rush him again while the crowd scattered.

They say the desk sergeant at the police station decided that day to make Ten to Ten a policeman, and Marabastad became a peaceful location.

That is the kind of story you do not have to believe to enjoy.

Another time, legend continues, the coal delivery man had some difficulty with his horse. He had a one-man horse-cart with which he delivered coal from door to door. On that occasion, the horse suddenly shied, perhaps having been pelted by mischievous boys with slings, and went dashing down the narrow avenue, scattering women with water tins on their heads. Just then Ten to Ten came round the corner. He caught the bridle of the horse and struggled to keep it still, being carried along a few yards himself. The horse reared and threatened to break away. Then Ten to Ten kicked it with his size 15 boot under the heart. The horse sagged, rolled over and died.

But it was not only for his violent exploits that we thrilled to him. Ten to Ten played soccer for the Police First Eleven; he played right fullback. For a giant his size he was remarkably swift, but it was his antics we loved. He would drop an oncoming ball dead before his own goalposts and, as the opponent's poor forward came rushing at him, he would quickly shift aside with the ball at the last moment, leaving the forward to go hurtling on his own momentum through the goalposts. Derisively he would call, 'Goal!' and the excited spectators would shout, 'Ten to Ten! Ten to Ten!'

Sometimes he would approach the ball ferociously with his rivals all about it, and he would make as if he was going to blast them ball and all. They would scuttle for cover, only to find that he had stopped the ball and was standing with one foot on it, grinning happily.

When he *did* elect to kick it, he had such powerful shots that the ball went from one end of the field to the other. Once, they say, he took a penalty kick. The ball went with such force that when the goalie tried to stop it, his hands were flayed and the deflected ball still went on to tear a string in the net.

'Ten to Ten!'

Yes, he had a sense of humour; and he was also the understanding kind. He knew about his great strength and seldom exercised it recklessly.

In Marabastad of those days there was a very quarrelsome little fellow called Shorty. He was about four feet six, but as they say, 'He buys tickey's beer and makes a pound's worth of trouble.' No one but Shorty ever really took his tantrums seriously, but people enjoyed teasing him for fun.

'Shorty,' they once told him, 'Ten to Ten's in that house

telling people that you're not a man, but just a sample.' Shorty boiled over. He strutted into the house with the comic little footsteps of the very short and found Ten to Ten sitting with a tin of beer in his hands.

He kicked the tin of beer out of Ten to Ten's hands, nearly toppling himself over in the process, and shouted, 'A sample of a man, eh? I'll teach you to respect your betters. Come outside and fight.' The others quickly signalled Ten to Ten that it was all a joke and he caught on. But Shorty was so aggrieved that he pestered Ten to Ten all afternoon.

At last Ten to Ten, tired of the sport, rose, lifted Shorty bodily off the ground and carried him down the street with a procession of cheering people behind them. Shorty was raging; he threw futile punches at Ten to Ten's chest. His dangling legs were kicking about furiously, but Ten to Ten carried him all the way to the police station.

It was a startled desk sergeant who suddenly found a midget landed on his desk, shouting, 'I'll kill him! I'll kill him!'

'What's this?' the sergeant wanted to know.

Wearily Ten to Ten explained, 'He says he wants to give me a fair fight.'

Shorty was fined ten bob and, when he came out of there, he turned to Ten to Ten disgustedly and spat, 'Coward!'

Ten to Ten walked with two other policemen, Constables Masemola and Ramokgopa, up First Avenue into glittering Boom Street. It was like suddenly walking out of an African slum into a chunk of the Orient. They strolled slowly up the tarred Boom Street, past the Empire Cinema. Now and then they would stop to look at the exotic foods in the window of some Indian shop and the pungent smells of eastern cooking and eastern toiletry would rise to their nostrils. Ahead, a hundred yards ahead, you could see the Africans who had no special permits to be out at night sorting themselves from the Indian and Coloured night crowds and dodging down some dark streets. They had long noticed the stalwart shadow of Ten to Ten coming up. He knew it too, but did not bother.

He reasoned inside himself that as long as they were scampering home, it was a form of respect for the Law. Unlike some of the other policemen who ferreted out Africans and delighted in chasing them down the road, to him, even when he caught one or two on the streets at night, it was enough to say, 'You there, home!' and as they fled before him his duty felt done.

Then they turned into the dark of Second Avenue of the location, away from where their eyes were guided by the blinking neons, into the murky streets where only their feet found the familiar way. It was silent, but Ten to Ten knew the residents were around, the silence was only because he was there. He was walking down the street, a presence that suddenly hushed these normally noisy people. In fact, he had heard their women as he entered the street calling down along it, 'Ten to Ten! Ten to Ten!'

It was not like the adulatory cheering on the soccer field, this calling of 'Ten to Ten!' This one had a long, dreary, plaintive note ... to carry it far along the street? Or to express heartfelt agony? In the field he felt their pride in him, the admiration for his wonderful physique, his skill and his sense of humour. The rapport between himself and the spectators who lined the field was delicious. There even the puniest of them would rush into the field after he had scored a goal, slap him on the back happily and say, 'Ai, but you, you Ten to Ten.'

He would come off the field and find a hero-worshipping youngster carrying his coat and pants to him and another pushing his glittering Hercules bicycle. The small boy would push out his robin chest and yell, 'Ten to Ten' unselfconsciously.

But here, people skulked behind tin shacks and wailed their misery at whatever perverse god crushed them, round about the hour of ten. Some of them were probably muttering in whispers even now as he passed. Had he not seen lower down the street a light suddenly go out in a house? It was probably a drinking house where they sat in the dark with their calabashes and tins trying to find their 'blind mouths', with the auntie of the house hissing importunately, 'Simeon, shut up, you fool, don't you know it's Ten to Ten?'

They passed a church and fancied they heard a rustling sound in the porch. They went to investigate. Out and past them bolted a boy and a girl. He mocked his shock after them, 'What, even in the House of the Lord!' They ran faster.

Fifth Street was empty and dark but before long they heard familiar grunting sounds. Ten to Ten signalled the other policemen to walk quietly. Off the street, hidden in an opening among tall grass, was a group of dice-players. They had formed a ring, inside which the candle was shielded from the breezes. The thrower would retreat a little from the ring, and shaking his dice in his bowled fist take a lunge forward, and cast them into the patch of light, giving a visceral grunt to coax his luck. Coins of the stake were lying in the centre.

Creeping low, Ten to Ten and his mates tiptoed up to them. They were so intent on the game that they heard nothing until suddenly he rose to his great height, like Mephistopheles out of the gloom, and bellowed, 'Ten to Ten!'

They splashed in all directions. One boy jumped into Ten to Ten and bounced back, falling to the ground. A policeman put a boot on his shoulder with just enough pressure to keep him there. Another chap never even got up, a rough hand had caught him by the neck. The boy who had nursed the candle tried to get away faster than his body would allow him and his feet kept slipping under him in his haste like a panicking dog's on a hard, smooth floor. He whimpered pointlessly, 'It's not me! It's not me!'

Ten to Ten just roared with Olympian laughter, 'Haw! Haw! Haw!'

When the boy finally took ground, he catapulted away. The other policemen brought the two detainees up to Ten to Ten; he did not trouble to question them, just re-lit the candle and held it in their frightened faces.

Then he said, 'Search them, Masemola. You know I'm only

interested in knives.'

Constable Masemola searched them but found no knives. In the pocket of one he found a little tin containing a condom. He held it up to Ten to Ten like the finger of a glove. 'Sies!' said Ten to Ten disgustedly, brushing aside Masemola's hand. Then to the boys, 'Off with you!' and they crashed through the tall grass into the location.

The other constables had picked up the coins from the ground and, while Masemola was still wondering aloud what those boys thought they knew about the use of condoms, Ten to Ten noticed the other constable pocketing the coins. Again, he just said, 'Sies!'

They went up Third Avenue, Ten to Ten thinking thoughts for which he could find no words ...

'Am I, perhaps, the only fool in this job? All the other policemen take bribes, intimidate shopkeepers, force half guilty conscience women to go to bed with them. Some beat up people needlessly, a few actually seem to enjoy the wanton slap, the unprovoked blow, the unreturnable kick for their own selves. Of course, it's seldom necessary for me to hit anybody. Before my bulk the runts fly. Maybe that's why. Maybe if I was little like these chaps I'd also want to push people around.

'But, really, you should hear these policemen grumble when the white sergeant barks at them in the charge office. Then they know they're black; that the white man is unreasonable, unjust, bossy, a bastard. But, God! See these chaps in the location on the beat. They treat their own people like ordure. And when the white man is with us on the beat, they surpass themselves. Damn that Ramokgopa! I felt so ashamed the other day when he hit a hopeless drunk with a baton until Sergeant Du Toit said, "That's enough now, Ramokgopa." God, I felt ashamed! The black man strikes, the white man says, "That's enough, now."

'And this business of making women sleep with you because you caught them with a drum of illicit beer. I can't understand it. If I want a piece of bottom – and, by God, now and then the fierce, burning pang stabs me, too – then I want the woman to want me too, to come alive under me, not to lie there like a dead fish. The thing's rape, man, however much she consented.

'What do I want in this job, anyway. It's a bastard of a job. Funny hours, low pay, strange orders that make no sense, violence, ever violence, and the daily spectacle of the degradation of my people. Well, I suppose it's a job. Otherwise I'd be with those workless fellows we corner every day and arrest for not having passes. Hell, if I hadn't taken this job, I'm sure I'd be in jail now. Jail? God, me, I'd long ago have been hanged for murder if some policeman handled me as our chaps manhandle these poor devils.

'But I have to work. I came here to work because I like to work. No, because back home in Tzaneen the people are starving, the rains haven't come these many years and the land is crying out, giving up the vain struggle to live – to push up one, little green blade, to justify herself – she lies just there like a barren, passionless woman seeing men hunger and die. No, but really because Mapula is waiting for me. Mapula? Ahhh! The memory stings me and I feel the subtle, nameless pain that only a big man knows. I can't cry ... I can't cry ...'

They came out of the location, again into Boom Street whose bright lights seemed to crackle into his twilight consciousness. They came out on to the bicycle shop.

A bicycle shop was supposed to repair bicycles and sell spare parts for them and there was always an upturned bicycle, one or other wheel missing, allegedly in the process of repair, outside the shop or at night in the window. But in Marabastad it was more of a music shop where the most raucous, the screechiest, the bansheest, the bawdiest cacophonies of township jazz bawled and caterwauled from the 78s inside to loudspeakers outside. 'We-Selina, go greet me your ma!' shrieked the lonesome son-in-law loud enough for his sweetheart, Selina, or indeed the mother-in-law herself, to hear him back in the Reserves.

Ten to Ten looked at his pocket watch. Twenty to twelve.

Odd, he thought, here was a Coloured girl dancing to music that was distinctly African township jazz – this chance thought was soon dispersed by the sight of the crowds that spilled from the Empire Cinema. Most of them were well-dressed Indian men with lovely Coloured girls; there were few Indian girls. A sprinkling of African men were in the crowd, but from their unalarmed expressions one could easily see that they had been to school and had the 'papers'.

As they strolled along the pavement the policemen saw an old Zulu, clad in a greenish khaki military overcoat, huddling over a glowing brazier. He was the Matshingilane – the nightwatchman. It was not clear which building he was guarding; probably several Indian bosses had chipped in to get him to look after the whole row of buildings. Lucky devil! Most times he slept well, safe in the knowledge that a policeman on the beat would stroll up and down watching the buildings for him.

'Poisa! Poisa! – Police! Police! They're killing an African man down there!'

Ten to Ten and his mates dashed down the street. They found a crowd of Indians pummelling a young African man. Ten to Ten barged into them like a bulldozer, pushing the crowd this way and that, until he got to the man on the ground.

'What's going on here?' he barked.

Scores of voices replied, 'He's a thief!'

'A pickpocket!'

'The lady's handbag!'

'He hit the gentleman first!'

'He bumped him!'

'And swore at him!'

'He's always robbing people!'

'We know him! We know him!'

Ten to Ten lifted the African from the ground. The man cowered before the enormous form over him.

'Well?' Ten to Ten asked.

'They lie,' was all the man could say for himself.

Somebody tried to grab at him but Ten to Ten pushed him away and pulled the victim towards himself, more protectively, saying, 'No, you don't.'

Then he addressed the crowd, 'Look here, I'm going to arrest this man and no one is going to take him away from me. No one, you hear?' He was quiet for a moment and looked around challengingly. Then he continued, 'Now, is there anybody who cares to lay a charge against him?'

There were murmurings, but no definite charge, someone called out weakly, 'But he's a thief.'

Ten to Ten said, 'All right, come forward and lay a charge.'

Instead, a hand again reached for the man. Ten to Ten released his charge for a moment to go after the owner of the hand, a half impulsive movement.

'Look out!' someone yelled and the crowd surged away. Ten to Ten spun round and saw that the African had drawn a long-bladed knife.

'Aw-right, come for me, you bastards!' he growled.

The savage blood leapt inside Ten to Ten. He lunged at the man like a black flash. If the knife had been shorter, he would have got it in the neck, but it was unwieldy and only slashed him across the shoulder.

'Ah!' soughed the fascinated crowd.

Ten to Ten caught the man's knife arm at the wrist and above the elbow, then brought it down on his upthrust knee. Crack! It snapped like a dry twig.

The sharp shriek curdled the night air and the knife went clattering to the pavement. The man went to the ground, whining, and the fury passed out of Ten to Ten.

Quietly, he said to the man, 'I could have killed you for that … knife.'

The crowd broke up in little groups into the night.

Ten to Ten said to Masemola, with a careless wave of the hand, 'Take him to De la Rey. I'm coming.'

He stood thinking, 'This was my bad night, the young, bloody fool!'

The Urchin

One sling of the braces would not keep up on the shoulder, just like one worm of pale green mucus kept crawling down the chestnut lip and would suddenly dart back like a timid creature. But Macala wore his long pants (surely someone's – someone older's castaway three-quarter jeans) with a defiant pride just ready to assault the rest of the known world. Other boys his ten year age only had short pants.

He looked up and down from Mafuta's Chinaman store along Victoria Road, Sophiatown, and he thought of how his day ought to begin. Mafuta's was no good: he kept two too ferocious dogs in his shop and fairly authenticated rumour had it that he also kept a gun that made a terrible noise. But the vistas up and down Victoria Road offered infinite possibilities for a man. To the left, there were queues on queues of half frightened, half foolish people who simply asked to be teased. Then Moosa's store with all those fruity, sweet things in the window: but they said Moosa trained at night with irons. Opposite, across Millar Street, there was a Chink butcher, but his counter was fenced off with wire, and Ooh! those cruel knives and hatchets. There must be a lot of money there for it to be protected so formidably. And, next to the butcher, the Bicycle Shop with its blaring jukebox: too roo roo roo tu! Too roo roo roo tu-tu! Where a passer-by girl would suddenly break into a dance step, seductive beyond her years.

All like that, up to Chang's, and from there just the denuded places the Demolition Squad had left in Sophiatown.

To the right Macala stared at Benghali House. The only double-storey building in the whole of Sophiatown. In front of it all sorts of pedlars met: sweet-potato sellers, maize sellers and sweet-reed sellers, African pimpled squash sellers, shoelace sellers – all bedamned whether or not the shopkeeper alone held a licence to sell anything.

Macala's eyes glittered as he saw the Ma-Ndebele women squatting in their timeless patience behind their huge dishes of maize cobs, dried morogo peanut cubes, wild fruits like marula, mahlatswa – things the urban African never sees on trees these days.

To Macala these women with their quaint and beaded necks and legs that made them look like colourful pythons were the fairest game.

He stepped off the veranda of Mafuta's shop, off the pavement, and sauntered swaggeringly towards those placid women in front of Benghali House. He was well aware that the street-corner loungers, enormous liars all of them, were watching him, thinking that the slightest move of Macala promised excitement and trouble.

He stopped in front of a Ndebele woman transfixed to her white dish, as if one with it, as if trade meant just being there at the strategic place and time: no bawling, no bartering, no bargaining.

'Dis – how much?' and that to Macala was English with a vengeance. She looked up at him with large baffled eyes, but before she spoke, Macala lifted his foot and trod on the edge of the dish, sending its contents churning out of it into the dust of Victoria Road's pavement. He shrieked with delight as he ran off.

What she hurled at him in virulent Ndebele may have been curses, prayers, lamentations. But to Macala it was reward enough, the kind of thing that proves the superiority of the townsman to these odd creatures from the country. And the passing generation's men and women shook their heads and muttered gloomily: 'The children of today, the children of today ...'

His momentum took him to the vegetable vendor just opposite Mafuta's. In fluid career, he seized the handle of the cart and whirled it round and up for the devil of it. Potatoes, onions, pumpkins, cabbages went swirling into the air and plump tomatoes squashed on the macadam. The khaki-coated vendor stood aghast a second before he broke into imprecations that shuddered even the sordid Sophiatown atmosphere. But Macala was away on his mischievous way.

He had passed the Fish and Chips too fast for another tilt and met his pals on the corner of Tucker and Victoria: Dipapang, Jungle and Boy-Boy. Together, they should have been 'Our Gang', but their organisation was not tight enough for that.

Boy-Boy's was the brain that germinated most of the junior devilry of the team, but he did not quite have Macala's impetuous courage of execution. He looked like a social worker's explanation of 'conditions in the slums': thin to malnourished, delinquent, undisciplined, dedicated to a future gallows. Yet his father was an important man and his mother a teacher. Jungle qualified by the ease with which he could talk of using a knife. In real big tsotsi fashion. Dipapang initiated nothing, thought nothing, was nothing, but always so willing to join in, try and finish anything the others cared to start.

'Heit, Macacix!' called Boy-Boy. 'How's it there?'

Macala suddenly felt in the mood for the jargon of the townships. The near-animal, amorphous, quick-shifting lingo that alarms farm-boys and drives cops to all branches of suspicion. But it marks the city slicker who can cope with all its vagaries.

'It's couvert under the corzet,' Macala replied, bobbing his head this way and that to the rhythm.

'Hai, man, bigshot, you must be the reel-reely outlaw in this town,' Boy-Boy parried and lunged.

'Naw,' Macala feinted, 'dis town, Softown's too small for me. I'll take Western and Corrie and Maclera and London, and smash them into a mashed potato.'

Boy-Boy fell for it. 'Whew!' he whistled, 'don't say you'll crowd me out!'

Macala took him by the throat and went in for the kill.

'Didn't I tell you, buster, to keep out of my country, or else ...'

He proceeded to carry out the menacing 'or else' by choking Boy-Boy and slowly tripping him over a leg he had slipped behind him until they rolled over as Boy-Boy fell, and tumbled into the gutter.

Boy-Boy gasped: 'Ah give up, boss, da country's yours.'

The mock battle was over and everybody laughed ... except Jungle. He was reputed to be 'serious' and that meant of the homicidal type. He sat there on the pavement drain with his mournful face, sharpening gratingly on the concrete his 3-Star jack-knife which from some hazy movie memory he called his 'gurkha'. As the laughter trailed off, he suddenly drawled: 'Have you guys heard that Mpedi was arrested yesterday?'

They stared at him in genuine stupefaction. Then Boy-Boy said: 'Yerrr! How'd it happen, Jungle?'

But Jungle was not one for elaborating a story. Very unsatisfactorily he said: 'Waal, he was drinking at de English Lady's joint ... and ... and dey got him.'

'You mean he didn't shoot it out? You mean dey took him just like dat? But I bet ya dey couldn't put handcuffs on Mpedi!' But Macala was very unhappy about the tame way the idol of the township was arrested.

Boy-Boy it was who made a story of it. 'Yerrr! But there is an outee.' He rose from the pavement and stood before the fascinated gaze of his pals. He stuck his thumbs into his belt and swayed his hips as he strutted up and down before them. Then he mimicked the bull-brained fearlessness of Mpedi, the mirror and form of almost all young Sophiatown, the clattering terror of men and the perennial exasperation of the police station across the road.

'Ya! Da room was full – full to da door. Clevers, bigshots, boozers, bamboos, coat-hangers, hole-diggers and bullets, blondes, figure 8s and capital Is, wash-planks and two-ton trucks. Da boys were in de stack and da dames were game ...

'Then Bura Mpedi stepped in, his eyes blood-red. The house went dead still. Ag man, Bura Mpedi, man. He stood there and looked left ... and looked right ... His man was not there. He stepped in some more. The house was dead. He grabbed a beer from the nearest table and slugged it from the bottle. Who would talk?' Boy-Boy's upper lip curled up on one side in utter contempt, 'Heh, who would talk!'

Macala and his pals were caught in Boy-Boy's electric pause. Even Jungle was aroused by this dramatic display of township bullycraft.

Boy-Boy's histrionics continued: 'Yerrrre! A drunk girl came from under a table and tried Mpedi for a drink. "Au, Bura Mpedi, give me a beer." Bura Mpedi put a boot on her shoulder and pushed her back under da table. Hai, man, hai man, dat outee is coward cool, man. And he hates cherry coat-hangers. But dat night his eyes were going all over looking for Mahlalela. Yeffies! If he'd caught Mahlalela dat night ...!'

Lifted by the wide-eyed admiration of his pals, Boy-Boy went on to surpass himself. He flung out his right arm recklessly and declared: 'But dat's nutting yet! You should have seen Bura Mpedi when dey sent four lean cops to come and take him. Payroll robbery, Booysens ... one thousand pound! Assault with GBH, Newlands ... three men down and out! Housebreakin' 'n thatha ... Lower Houghton!

'Dey came, man dey came. Four cops, two had guns, two had small inches (batons). Dey surrounded da joint in Gibson Street and dey called out to him to give up. Dey didn't know Mpedi with moon-wash in his brains and a human intestine round his waist. He drew his point-three-five and his forty-five and he came out shooting. Rwah! Da two cops with small inches ducked into a shebeen nearby and ordered themselves a ha' nip brandy. One with da gun ran down Gibson Street for reinforces. Da last cop took a corner and decided to shoot it out with Mpedi. But da bullets came so fast he never got a chance to poke out a shot.

'Hee-e-e, I tell you Mpedi was da outee.' Then still carried forward by the vibrance of his enthusiasm, Boy-Boy rounded off his dramatisation by backing away slowly as he fired off imaginary guns and barked: 'Twah! Twah! Twah!'

But the elation that had swelled up in Macala was now shot through with envy. 'How come,' he grumbled, 'da cops got him so easy now?' Yet what really worried him was that he knew how far he was beneath the fabulous Mpedi; that, even in his own weight division, he could not make such an awe-inspiring impression. He was not even as good an actor as Boy-Boy to recount and represent the exploits of the almighties. He looked at Boy-Boy bitterly and told himself: I'll beat his brains out if he gets smart with me.

It was Jungle who wrenched him out of his sour reverie. 'Boys, I think we should go finish off da Berliners,' Jungle said prosaically.

A flash of fear leapt into Boy-Boy's eyes, for he knew this meant war. Macala was himself a bit scared, but seeing the fear in Boy-Boy, he screwed his heart through a hole too small for it.

And Jungle's gurkha went on scraping the pavement concrete, screech-screech! screech-screech!

'Come ahn, let's go,' Macala suddenly decided.

They swaggered along Victoria Road, filling it from pavement to pavement as if they were a posse. Silent. Full of purpose. Deliberately grim. Boys and girls scampered for cover. Grown-ups stepped discreetly out of their way. Only the bigger tsotsis watched them with pride and shouted encouragements like: Da men who rule da town! Tomorrow's outees!

On the corner of Meyer Street they broke up a ring of young dicers and forced them to join up. Along the way they collected non-schoolgoing loafers who lounged against shop walls; blue-jeaned youngsters who twisted the arms of schoolgirls in rough love; odd job boys who ran errands for shopkeepers; truants, pick-pockets, little thugs within their age limit – the lot.

By the time they turned into Edith Street they were a miniature army of hell-bent ruffians. Macala led them and felt the strange thrill of the force behind him. He chose Edith Street because it rose into a rocky hill with plenty of stones for ammunition, and dropped suddenly into that part of Sophiatown they called Berlin, where the walls were smeared with crude swastikas.

Macala split his men into two groups. Those with thick, bronze buckle belts were to go under Jungle through a cut in the row of houses precariously perched on huge boulders.

The excitement chopped Macala's breath into collops as he gave out his instructions. 'You boys get dem from de back. You start de war. When dey come running up Edward Road, dey'll meet us. Use dat butcher of yours, Uncle Jungle.'

Jungle gave one of his rare smiles and his men took position.

Macala and his group, first placing a sentinel on the hilltop, slowly clambered down the rocks and waited for Jungle to get around.

Though going into the den of the enemy, Jungle did not find it difficult to rout them. There was a biggish group of them playing dice in the usual ring and, when he swooped upon them, they instinctively thought it was the police and dashed up Edward Road, sticks and buckle belts raining on their heads.

Jungle himself had chosen a heftily built fellow and was stabbing at him as he ran. Boy-Boy was later to describe it graphically: 'Yerre! Dat guy just wouldn't fall. Jungle had him – zip! But he ran on. Jungle caught him again in the neck – zip! He stumbled and trotted on his hands and feet. Jungle got him in the buttock – zip! But, yerre! He just wouldn't fall!'

Before the Berliners could rally and make a stand, they had run into Macala's stone-throwing division. Though very one-sided, the fight became fierce. The Berliners were now fighting and, because they were trapped and because they had to fight with their bare hands most of the time, they became young devils from the playgrounds of Hell.

Stones and all sorts of other missiles were hurled in all

directions. Knives were brandished and plunged, big-buckled belts were swung in whistling arcs, arms were flailed in the centre of the imbroglio with desperate savagery. Women screamed, shops closed, traffic diverted itself. Now and then, a blood-bespattered boy would stagger off the street to a side wall just to sit down and watch. Too done in to flee.

Then suddenly came the shrill warning cry, 'Arrara! Arrarayii!' The action stopped almost as abruptly as those ancient films which froze in mid-motion and transfixed the movement into a photograph. And just as suddenly after, they scattered all pell-mell. When the police van came round the corner, it was impossible to decide which flee-ers to pursue. For, now, everybody was running up and down and off the streets. The scores of small boys, ordinary pedestrians who had just alighted upon the scene, fah-fee runners with full-blown cheeks a-chomping the incriminating tickets of their illicit lottery; everybody was running. In Sophiatown you do not stop to explain to the police that you had nothing to do with it, or that you knew some of the culprits and could help the police.

The mobile squad were satisfied with merely clearing the street.

Breathless and bruised, Macala found himself at the open commonage called Makouvlei, adjacent to Waterval Hospital, which served as the waste dumps to the city and 'golf course' to those Africans who went in for the sport of leisure. Macala knew that most of his gang would sooner or later find their way there. He sat on a mound of ash, gasping heavily.

By the time Boy-Boy arrived there, he had regained his breath and was pitching chalky, burnt-out pebbles rather pointlessly. Jungle came, for once, apparently, in his seventh heaven. Dipapang, too, grinned happily though his shirt had been torn down and hung like a hula. A few other stragglers from the Black Caps joined them, and then came the News. News that oddly took the shape of 'They say'.

'Dey say,' announced one urchin, 'dat one of de Berliners

is dead.'

Stultifying fright seized them all. Some small boy broke out crying. Macala had trouble with a choking clod in his throat.

'Dey say,' came in another boy, 'de Berliners are going to call in de Big Berliners.'

'Agh,' grunted Macala in contempt, 'we'll go'n tell Bura Shark.'

'Dey say de cops're going to round us all up tonight.'

Despite all their bravado, all their big-shot stances and their blistering contempt for cops and the law, there is one thing that this knighthood really fears, and it was expressed by a crackling of interjections from each according to his own lights: 'Six lashes and reformatory!'

'De cane and off to a farm!'

'Cuts with a light cane and no fine!'

Someone elaborated the procedure by filling in the gory details: 'Dey say, two huge cops hold you down over a big bench an' you got nothin' on. You can't move. Now, maybe de magistrate he said: "Six cuts." Dat's nothin'. If you cry, for every one you get two. An' dose cops who give de lashes, dey train for you, dey pick up weightlifting for you, dey grip a grip all day for you. Den when de other cops got you on de bench, an' you can't move, an' you don't want to cry, de lashing cop he takes de cane, he swishes it over his head, one-two-three, whish! De tattoo jumps up on your buttocks.

'Dey say, he den goes to sit down, light a cigarette and talks with de other cops. Den he comes again. One of de cops holding you turns your head so you can see de lashing cop coming. He swishes de cane, one-two-three, whish! 'Nother tattoo comes up, dis time with blood. Red blood from your buttocks. He goes for 'nother puff at his cigarette, or maybe he looks for his tea dis time.

'He comes again. Dis time he sneezes his nose on your buttocks, and makes joke how black buttocks is tough. He swishes de cane, one-two-three, whish! If you don't cry, maybe you get your six lashes straight. But if you cry, only just Maye

Babo – oh-ho-ho! ...

'An' dey say, sometimes after you get lashes, six days, two weeks you can't sit in de bus, you give your seat to de aunties. Hai, dat cane dey keep in de salt water when nobody get lashes!'

By that time the horror of the prospect had seeped through every delinquent soul. It was Macala who spoke first.

He said determinedly: 'Me, I'm not going home tonight.'

But Boy-Boy did not like the idea. He knew that his mother would not rest until she had found out where he was. Worse still, she might even go ask the police to help her find him. 'Naw, Macacix, I'm going home. I don't like cops catching me when my ma is not there. I'm going home.'

As he walked away, the whole little gang suddenly broke up and walked home their different ways. Macala went frantic with panic. With consternation twisted in his face and his arms floating like a blind man's in front of him, he looked half comic as he stood on that mount of ash.

'Hey, hey, you guys won't leave me alone. We're de boys ...'

He heard a sound of impatience behind him: 'Aargh! Let them go, Macala.' He turned round and reeled unsteadily as he saw Jungle standing there, not looking frightened at all.

'Wh-what you going to do, Jungle?'

Jungle took out his gurkha and scraped it across his palm from left to right, right to left. Then he said: 'I'm going home, Macala,' and that mournful expression crept across his countenance. 'And when de cops come to get me tonight ...' He made an ugly motion with his knife under his chin. He walked away with the slow, lanky movement of the gawky body of his.

By the time Macala decided to leave Makouvlei, it was getting dark. But he knew where he was going. Rather unnecessarily, he skulked along the fences of the street, looking this way and that. Now and then he would petrify at the zoom of a passing car or duck into an alley when headlights bore goldenly through the dark of the street. But ultimately he reached the open space where Gerty, Bertha and Toby Streets used to be. He saw the dark building for which he was headed. He ran forward and stopped in front of it, but this side of the street. Slowly now. Somewhere here there is a nightwatchman, a Zulu with a thick black beard and barbel moustache, black uniform and black face that rubbed him out of sight in the dark and a gnarled knobkerrie known to have split skulls.

But Macala knew where the corrugated iron fence had snarled out a lip of entrance for him. He went on his hands and knees and crawled away from the immense double gate towards this entrance. He found it and coiled himself inside. He knew there were stacks of corrugated iron in this timber yard, and if he touched them the racket would alert the nightwatchman. So he did not go far, just nestled himself near his exit.

A little breeze was playing outside, hasting a piece of paper down the street, and now and then a bus or lorry would thunder by. But Macala slept, occasionally twitching in the hidden mechanics of sleep. Far from where he could hear, a woman's voice was calling stridently: 'Mac-a-a-ala! Mac-a-a-a-la! Hai, that child will one day bring me trouble.'

The Suit

Five-thirty in the morning, and the candlewick bedspread frowned as the man under it stirred. He did not like to wake his wife lying by his side – as yet; so he crawled up and out by careful peristalsis. But before he tiptoed out of his room with shoes and socks under his arm, he leaned over and peered at the sleeping serenity of his wife: to him a daily matutinal miracle.

He grinned and yawned simultaneously, offering his wordless Te Deum to whatever gods for the goodness of life; for the pure beauty of his wife; for the strength surging through his willing body; for the even, unperturbed rhythms of his passage through days and months and years – it must be – to heaven.

Then he slipped soundlessly into the kitchen. He flipped aside the curtain of the kitchen window and saw outside a thin drizzle, the type that can soak one to the skin and that could go on for days and days. He wondered, head aslant, why the rain in Sophiatown always came in the morning when workers have to creep out of their burrows; and then blistering heat waves during the day when messengers have to run errands all over; and then at how even the rain came back when workers knock off and have to scurry home.

He smiled at the odd caprice of the heavens, and tossed his head at the naughty incongruence, as if: 'Ai, but the gods!'

From behind the kitchen door he removed an old rain cape, peeling off in places, and swung it over his head. He dashed for the lavatory, nearly slipping in a pool of muddy water, but he reached the door. Aw, blast, someone had made it before him. Well, that is the toll of staying in a yard where twenty, thirty other people have to share the same lean-to. He was dancing and burning in that climactic moment when trouser-fly will not come wide soon enough. He stepped round the lavatory and watched the streamlets of rainwater quickly wash away the jet of tension that spouted from him. That infinite after-relief. Then he dashed back to his kitchen. He grabbed the old baby bathtub hanging on a nail on the side of a wall under the slight shelter of the gutterless roof edge. He opened a large wooden box and quickly filled the bathtub with coal. Then he inched his way back to the kitchen door and inside.

He was huh-huh-huhing one of those fugitive tunes that cannot be bidden, but often just occur and linger, naggingly, in his head, and the fire he was making soon licked up cheerfully, in mood with his contentment.

He had a trick for these morning chores. While the fire in the old stove warmed up, the kettle humming on it, he gathered and laid ready the things he would need for the day: briefcase and the files that go with it; the book that he was reading currently; the letters of his lawyer of a boss which he usually posted before he reached the office; his wife's and his own dry cleaning slips for the Sixty-Minutes; his lunch tin solicitously prepared the night before by his attentive wife. And, today, the battered rain cape. By the time the kettle on the stove sang (before it actually boiled), he poured water from it into a wash basin, refilled the kettle and replaced it on the stove. Then he washed himself carefully: across the eyes, along the nose bridge, up and down the cheeks, around the ears, under, in and out the armpits, down the torso and in between the legs. This ritual was thorough, though no white man a-complaining of the smell of wogs knows anything about it. Then he dressed himself fastidiously. By this time he was ready to prepare breakfast.

Breakfast! How he enjoyed taking round a tray of warm breakfast to his wife, cuddled in bed. To appear there in his supremest immaculacy, tray in hand, when his wife comes out of ether to behold him. These things we blacks want to do for our own ... not fawningly for the whites for whom we bloody well got to do it. He felt, he denied that he was one of those who believed in putting his wife in her place even if she was a good wife. Not he.

Matilda, too, appreciated her husband's kindness, and only put her foot down when he offered to wash up also. 'Off with you,' she scolded him on his way.

At the bus stop he was a little sorry to see that jovial old Maphikela was in a queue for a bus ahead of him. He would miss Maphikela's raucous laughter and uninhibited, bawdy conversations in fortissimo. Maphikela hailed him nevertheless. He thought he noticed hesitation in the old man, and slight clouding of his countenance, but the old man shouted back at him, saying that he would wait for him at the terminus in town.

Philemon always considered this morning trip to town with garrulous old Maphikela as his daily bulletin. All the township news was generously reported by loud-mouthed heralds and spiritedly discussed by the bus at large. Of course, 'news' included views on bosses (scurrilous), the Government (rude), Ghana and Russia (idolatrous), America and the West (sympathetically ridiculing), boxing (bloodthirsty). But it was always stimulating and surprisingly comprehensive for so short a trip. And there was no law of libel.

Maphikela was standing under one of those token bus stop shelters that never keep out rain or wind or sunheat. Philemon easily located him by his noisy ribbing of some office boys in their khaki green uniforms. They walked together into town, but from Maphikela's suddenly subdued manner Philemon gathered there was something serious coming up. Maybe a loan.

Eventually Maphikela came out with it.

'Son,' he said sadly, 'if I could've avoided this, believe you me I would. But my wife is nagging the spice out of my life for not talking to you about it.'

It just did not become blustering old Maphikela to sound so grave and Philemon took compassion upon him. 'Go ahead, dad,' he said generously, 'you know you can talk to me about anything.'

The old man gave a pathetic smile. 'We-e-ell, it's not really any of our business ... er ... but my wife felt ... you see. Damn it all! I wish these women would not snoop around so much.' Then he rushed it. 'Anyway, it seems there's a young man who's going to visit your wife every morning ... ah ... for these last bloomin' three months. And that wife of mine swears by her heathen gods you don't know a thing about it.'

It was not quite like the explosion of a devastating bomb. It was more like the critical breakdown in an infinitely delicate piece of mechanism. From outside the machine just seemed to have gone dead. But deep in its innermost recesses, menacing electrical flashes were leaping from coil to coil, and hot, viscous molten metal was creeping up on the fuel tanks ...

Philemon heard gears grinding and screaming into gears in his head ...

'Dad,' he said hoarsely, 'I ... I have to go back home.'

He turned round and did not hear old Maphikela's anxious: 'Steady, son. Steady, son.'

The bus ride home was a torture of numb dread and suffocating despair. Though the bus was now emptier, Philemon suffered crushing claustrophobia. There were immense washerwomen whose immense bundles of soiled laundry seemed to baulk and menace him. From those bundles crept miasmata of sweaty intimacies that sent nauseous waves up and down from his viscera. Then the wild swaying of the bus as it negotiated Mayfair Circle hurtled him sickeningly from side to side. Some of the younger women shrieked delightedly to the driver: Fuduga ... Stir the pot! as he swung his steering wheel this way and that. Normally the crazy tilting of the bus gave him a prickling exhilaration. But now ...

He felt like getting out of there, screamingly, elbowing everything out of his way. He wished this insane trip were over, and then again he recoiled at the thought of getting home. He made a tremendous resolve to gather in all the torn, tingling threads of his nerves contorting in the raw. By a merciless act of will, he kept them in subjugation as he stepped out of the bus back in the Victoria Road terminus, Sophiatown.

The calm he achieved was tense ... but he could think now ... he could take a decision ...

With almost boyishly innocent urgency, he rushed through his kitchen into his bedroom. In the lightning flash that the eye can whip, he saw it all ... the man beside his wife ... the chestnut arm around her neck ... the ruffled candlewick bedspread ... the suit across the chair. But he affected not to see.

He opened the wardrobe door and, as he dug into it, he cheerfully spoke to his wife: 'Fancy, Tilly, I forgot to take my pass. I had already reached town and was going to walk up to the office. If it hadn't been for wonderful old Mr Maphikela.'

A swooshing noise of violent retreat and the clap of his bedroom window stopped him. He came from behind the wardrobe door and looked out from the open window. A man clad only in vest and underpants was running down the street. Slowly, he turned round and contemplated ... the suit.

Philemon lifted it gingerly under his arm and looked at the stark horror in Matilda's eyes. She was now sitting up in bed. Her mouth twitched, but her throat raised no words.

'Ha,' he said, 'I see we have a visitor,' indicating the blue suit. 'We really must show some of our hospitality. But first, I must phone my boss that I can't come to work today ... mmmm-er, my wife's not well. Be back in a moment, then we can make arrangements.' He took the suit along.

When he returned he found Matilda weeping. He dropped the suit beside her on the bed, pulled up the chair, turned it round so that its back came in front of him, sat down, brought his chin on his folded arms before him and waited for her.

After a while the convulsions of her shoulders ceased. She saw a smug man with an odd smile and meaningless inscrutability in his eyes. He spoke to her with very little noticeable emotion in his voice; if anything, with a flutter of

119

humour.

'We have a visitor, Tilly.' His mouth curved ever so slightly. 'I'd like him to be treated with the greatest of consideration. He will eat every meal with us and share all we have. Since we have no spare room, he'd better sleep in here. But the point is, Tilly, that you will meticulously look after him. If he vanishes or anything else happens to him ...' A shaft of evil shot from his eye ... 'Matilda, I'll kill you.'

He rose from the chair and looked with incongruous supplication at her. He told her to put the fellow in the wardrobe for the time being. As she passed him to get the suit, he turned to go. She ducked frantically and he stopped.

'You don't seem to understand me, Matilda. There's to be no violence in this house if you and I can help it. So, just look after that suit.' He went out.

He went to the Sophiatown Post Office which is placed on the exact latitude between Sophiatown and the white man's surly Westdene. He posted his boss's letters and walked to the beer hall at the tail end of Western Native Township. He had never been inside it before, but somehow the thunderous din laved his bruised spirit. He stayed there all day.

He returned home for supper ... and surprise. His dingy little home had been transformed, and the stern masculinity it had hitherto received had been wiped away, to be replaced by anxiously feminine touches here and there. There were even gay, colourful curtains swirling in the kitchen window. The old-fashioned coal stove gleamed in its blackness. A clean, chequered oilcloth on the table. Supper ready.

Then she appeared in the doorway of the bedroom. Heavens! Here was the woman he had married; the young, fresh cocoa-coloured maid who had sent rushes of emotion shuddering through him. And the dress she wore brought out all the girlishness of her, hidden so long beneath German print. But no hint of coquettishness, although she stood in the doorway and slid her arm up the jamb, and shyly slanted her head to the other shoulder. She smiled weakly.

What makes a woman like this experiment with adultery? he wondered.

Philemon closed his eyes and gripped the seat of his chair on both sides as some overwhelming, undisciplined force sought to catapult him towards her. For a moment some essence glowed fiercely within him, then sank back into itself and died ...

He sighed and smiled sadly back at her.

'I'm hungry, Tilly.'

The spell snapped and she was galvanised into action. She prepared his supper with dextrous hands that trembled a little only when they hesitated in mid-air. She took her seat opposite him, regarded him curiously, clasped her hands waiting for his prayer, but in her heart she murmured some other, much more urgent prayer of her own.

'Matilda!' he barked. 'Our visitor!' The sheer savagery with which he cracked at her jerked her up, but only when she saw the brute cruelty in his face did she run out of the room, toppling the chair behind her.

She returned with the suit on a hanger, stood there quivering like a feather. She looked at him with helpless dismay. The demoniacal rage in his face was evaporating, but his heavy breathing still rocked his thorax above the table, to and fro.

'Put a chair, there.' He indicated with a languid gesture of his arm. She moved like a ghost as she drew a chair to the table.

'Now seat our friend at the table ... no, no, not like that. Put him in front of the chair, and place him on the seat so that he becomes indeed the third person.'

Philemon went on relentlessly: 'Dish up for him. Generously. I imagine he hasn't had a morsel all day, the poor devil.'

Now, as consciousness and thought seeped back into her, her movements revolved so that always she faced this man who had changed so spectacularly. She started when he rose to open the window and let in some air.

She served the suit. The act was so ridiculous that she

carried it out with a bitter sense of humiliation. He came back to sit down and plunge into his meal. No grace was said for the first time in this house. With his mouth full, he indicated by a toss of his head that she should sit down in her place. She did so, glanced at her plate, and the thought occurred to her that someone, after a long famine, was served a sumptuous supper, but as the food reached her mouth it turned to sawdust. Where had she heard it?

Matilda could not eat. She suddenly broke into tears.

Philemon took no notice of her weeping. After supper he casually gathered the dishes and started washing up. He flung a dry cloth at her without saying a word. She rose and went to stand by his side, drying up. But for their wordlessness, they seemed a very devoted couple.

After washing up, he took the suit and turned to her. 'That's how I want it every meal, every day.' Then he walked into the bedroom.

So it was. After that first breakdown Matilda began to feel that her punishment was not too severe, considering the heinousness of her crime. She tried to put a joke into it. But by slow, unconscious degrees, the strain nibbled at her. Philemon did not harass her much more, so long as the ritual with the confounded suit was conscientiously followed.

Only once, he got one of his malevolent brainwaves. He got it into his head that 'our visitor' needed an outing. Accordingly the suit was taken to the dry cleaners during the week and, come Sunday, they had to take it out for a walk. Both Philemon and Matilda dressed for the occasion. Matilda had to carry the suit on its hanger over her back and the three of them strolled leisurely along Ray Street. They passed the church crowd in front of the famous Anglican Mission of Christ the King. Though the worshippers saw nothing unusual in them, Matilda felt, searing through her, red-hot needles of embarrassment, and every needlepoint was a public eye piercing into her degradation.

But Philemon walked casually on. He led her down Ray

Street, turned into Main Road. He stopped often to look into shop windows or to greet a friend passing by. They went up Toby Street, turned into Edward Road, and back home. To Philemon the outing was free of incident, but to Matilda it was one long, excruciating incident.

At home he grabbed a book on Abnormal Psychology, flung himself into a chair and calmly said to her: 'Give the old chap a rest, will you, Tilly?'

In the bedroom, Matilda said to herself that things could not go on like this. She thought of how she could bring the matter to a head with Philemon, have it out with him once and for all. But the memory of his face, that first day she had forgotten to entertain the suit, stayed her. She thought of running away. Where to? Home? What could she tell her old-fashioned mother had happened between Philemon and her? All right, run away clean then. She thought of many young married girls who were divorcees now, who had won their freedom.

What had happened to Staff Nurse Kakile? That woman drank heavily now, and when she got drunk, the boys of Sophiatown passed her around and called her the Cesspot.

Matilda shuddered.

An idea struck her. There were still decent, married women around Sophiatown. She remembered how, after the schools had been forced to close with the advent of Bantu Education, Father Harringay of the Anglican Mission had organised Cultural Clubs. One, she seemed to remember, was for married women. If only she could lose herself in some cultural activity, find ablution for her conscience in some doing good; that would blur her blasted home life, would restore her self-respect. After all, Philemon had not broadcast her disgrace abroad ... nobody knew; not one of Sophiatown's vicious slander-mongers suspected how vulnerable she was. She must go and see Mrs Montjane about joining a Cultural Club. She must ask Philemon now if she might ... she must ask him nicely.

She got up and walked into the other room where Philemon

was reading quietly. She dreaded disturbing him, did not know how to begin talking to him ... they had talked so little for so long. She went and stood in front of him, looking silently upon his deep concentration. Presently he looked up with a frown on his face.

Then she dared: 'Phil, I'd like to join one of those Cultural Clubs for married women. Would you mind?'

He wrinkled his nose and rubbed it between thumb and index finger as he considered the request. But he had caught the note of anxiety in her voice, and thought he knew what it meant.

'Mmmm,' he said, nodding. 'I think that's a good idea. You can't be moping around here all day. Yes, you may, Tilly.' Then he returned to his book.

That Cultural Club idea was wonderful. She found women like herself, with time (if not with tragedy) on their hands, engaged in wholesome, refreshing activities. The atmosphere was cheerful and cathartic. They learned things and they did things. They organised fêtes, bazaars, youth activities, sport, music, self-help and community projects. She got involved in committees, meetings, debates, conferences. It was for her a whole new venture into humancraft and her personality blossomed. Philemon gave her all the rein she wanted.

Now, abiding by that silly ritual at home seemed a little thing ... a very little thing ...

Then one day she decided to organise a little party for her friends and their husbands. Philemon was very decent about it. He said it was all right. He even gave her extra money for it. Of course, she knew nothing of the strain he himself suffered from his mode of castigation.

There was a week of hectic preparation. Philemon stepped out of its cluttering way as best he could. So many things seemed to be taking place simultaneously. New dresses were made. Cakes were baked, three different orders of meat prepared: beef for the uninvited chancers; mutton for the normal guests; turkey and chicken for the inner pith of the club's core. To Philemon, it looked as if Matilda planned to feed the multitude on the mount with no aid of miracles.

On the Sunday of the party Philemon saw Matilda's guests. He was surprised by the handsome grace with which she received them. There was a long table with enticing foods and flowers and serviettes. Matilda placed all her guests round the table and the party was ready to begin in the mock formal township fashion. Outside a steady rumble of conversation went on where the human odds and ends of every Sophiatown party had their 'share'.

Matilda caught the curious look on Philemon's face. He tried to disguise his edict when he said: 'Er ... the guest of honour.' But Matilda took a chance. She begged: 'Just this once, Phil.' He became livid. 'Matilda!' he shouted, 'get our visitor!' Then with incisive sarcasm: 'Or are you ashamed of him?'

She went ash grey; but there was nothing for it but to fetch her albatross. She came back and squeezed a chair into some corner and placed the suit on it. Then she slowly placed a plate of food before it. For a while the guests were dumbfounded. Then curiosity flooded in. They talked at the same time. 'What's the idea, Philemon?' ... 'Why must she serve a suit?' ... 'What's happening?' Some just giggled in a silly way. Philemon carelessly swung his head towards Matilda. 'You better ask my wife. She knows the fellow best.'

All interest beamed upon poor Matilda. For a moment she could not speak, all enveloped in misery. Then she said, unconvincingly: 'It's just a game that my husband and I play at mealtime.'

They roared with laughter. Philemon let her get away with it.

The party went on and, every time Philemon's glare sent Matilda scurrying to serve the suit each course, the guests were no end amused by the persistent mock seriousness with which this husband and wife played out their little game. Only, to Matilda, it was no joke; it was a hot poker down her throat. After the party, Philemon went off with one of the guests who had promised to show him a joint 'that sells genuine stuff, boy, genuine stuff'.

Reeling drunk, late that Sabbath, he crashed through his kitchen door, onwards to his bedroom. Then he saw her.

They have a way of saying in the argot of Sophiatown: 'Cook out of the head!' signifying that someone was impacted with such violent shock that whatever whiffs of alcohol still wandered through his head were instantaneously evaporated and the man stood sober before stark reality.

There she lay, curled as if, just before she died, she begged for a little love, implored some implacable lover to cuddle her a little ... just this once ... just this once more.

In screwish anguish Philemon cried: 'Tilly!'

Quoth He

One sultry afternoon, all the committees asiesta and just an angel or two fluttering through the empyrean, with knitted brow and hands clasped athwart his bottom, God wandered into his arbour, and thought.

Quoth he to himself: *did I try the African?*

Nice little bit that, a coupla centuries of slavery, years of bondage and that brilliant touch – the dab of colour. Brilliant. Magnifique. Brought all the crudities and brutalities of the centuries, from Satan to Verwoerd, to this. But consider I played a mite too rough with this kaffir boy, the only boy who really believed in me. So Jonah – he proved my point, though.

But too much of frivolous moods have caught me these days. French Revolutions, St Bartholomew Massacres, a Borgia here, a Nero there, a Medici or a Shaka or a Machiavel, those are peripheries of my imagination. Other ones are Schweitzers, Curies, Socrates, Christs. God (pardon, 'Satan'), how the hell can I make the African palpitate? Or will he exact it of me? Would he dare?

But he fascinates me. Fancy the throb of jungle drums – sounds that all of us mistook for granted are part of the great heart of nature in its most ordinary acts of respiration, mastication, fornication and death. Death never perturbed me, nor pain, nor suffering, cruelty, nor depredation. Nor injustice, neither. But sorrow, perhaps. Or ignorance. That is why I never could abide the silly prayers they hurl from their abysses to the threshold of my throne. Having granted them in the first throes of creation Intelligence, Manhood, Discontent and an exuberant nature, they still come whimpering to me: 'Give us this day.'

But yes, the African fascinates me. Seeking expression like the rest, he still finds novel ways of addressing me. He prances and dances; he threatens and trembles; he grunts and groans; and some of the time he ingenuously lifts a smile to me as his claw is upon his victim, even as he mutters: 'Forgive us our trespasses.'

What ails me, though, is that this genuine child of nature is learning the game of those others. He learns to equivocate, prevaricate and find a sweet song for the philosophy that is blood or for the religion that is dust. Black bitter pity it is. For I consider that he has so much to give in laughter and human understanding and those fleet-secret-subtle movements of soul. His wrath is lectric, his passion is thunderous, his tenderness is lachrymal, as if he strives to tell the world: let us not be ashamed to be human. That world that replies, tartly: don't be an ass.

Oddly, though, he does not seriously inject his colour into the affairs of his time, drop by drop, to make a venomous crucible. Everywhere he seeks brotherhood. There too, where he meets ingratitude's stench or the evil hand that smites him, his protest is the outcry for outraged humanity. Not, not as yet, the call to vengeance. Strue's God, he has cause to want to strike down hemispheres. He has enough piled up rage in some hidden bile of his to poison a score of centuries, yet all the child asks for is justice. Astounding!

That even I, his creator, should find it astonishing.

The creature is either a fool or some part of divine stuff pilfered from me. For when I decree destitution and degradation to him, somehow he survives and continues to exist in defiance of the laws of my Nature. And times there were when in omnipotent rage I ordained for him annihilation, and the worm said: 'Ordure!' and continued to crawl across the flower of my life. Methinks he deserves to live; more than that, he warrants a wreath, a crown, a halo. But I'm accustomed to make men earn my rewards. How make an exception of him?

If only he would exert himself. It matters not to me what

methods, moral or supramoral, of his age he elects, so long as he flexes his muscles and sweeps his arm across his horizon and, looking back upon the devastation, he is able to say: 'Here passed a man.'

But it seems he wants to do good. Well, let him. Rather let me give him that thirty-three and a third per cent agreed upon for a break. His trainer and manager and lawyers are his own indaba. I'll give him the Sixties. If he can't work it out in that span, to hell with him. Or can he scrounge a decade or two from me? Hee-hee, let him try!

Still, I was honestly interested in that plea for coexistence that this louse offers the lions. It has just that tang of integrity I'd hope some human would hit upon. Will this one too make a holy thing turn to ash in my grateful mouth? I suppose, working with stuff like that, I've got to take a chance. But Jesus, it fascinates me, the chances that I take in trying to make a Universe work! Why the hell don't I do things myself, seeing how clumsily my creatures carry out a matter so simple as rolling one dung-heap from here to there?

One would have thought it's elementary just to get humans of the same make and prejudice to live sensibly together. But I've had to go out of my way to create an African, just to make people wonder how they bloody well had to. Well, they bloody well have to.

There were times in a desperate mood when I felt like drawing in my claws and crushing this infamous planet. But even I can't always indulge all my tantrums. After all, I'm God, ain't I? So be it. So let the African have his chance. But, so help me, if he goes like the rest …

I make no mistakes. I *know*. I know this black bastard is going to let me down like the rest of them. But then, like the rest of them, I ask the most of him, too. If he can't make it, if he can't make himself in the puny standards that humans set themselves, well: *merde*!

So, from as of now, I don't allow a literature, a philosophy, an art, a religion to establish itself without due regard to the common existence of all men. I know, I know; my learned friend from under need not sneer and suggest that the African has been made by his learned friend from hither to be thus. But I'm giving him a greater break. The ass won't understand that it's a greater break if it's under more trying conditions. Well, blast it – it's because I want him to be more man that I've made him so much slave. I've given him patience for I want him to build up solidity for the special trial I've planned for him. The poor bastard may make it or disintegrate. What is it to me that a heel crushes a worm, that a bullet snuffs out a man, that a stroke of lightning or a mishap or a mispigmentation maligns a soul. The chance, it is, the chance that I give them all. And where they can't see that it's a chance I gave them, let them make, take, fake their own chance. Still they have my nod.

But before their little day is over, I'd like to hear the song of Africa. Let them crane the necks and lift their voices, in woe or in throe or in thunderous no, let them but speak, and I shall hear.

Let them just speak, and not editorialise, themselves into my heart.

Through Shakespeare's Africa

Anthony Sampson, sometime editor of *Drum*, was perhaps the first person to remark that the turbulence of urban African life was like the stage of Shakespeare's Elizabethan world – the action, the passion, the lasciviousness, the high drama, the violence and then: 'Exeunt with corpses.' One supposes that violence as life's ordinary stuff can be found in many other communities over the world. I would not be surprised to learn that in parts of Chicago of an evening saunter, even today, a couple could be coshed and robbed; that in Rome or Venice a jealous lover still doesn't hesitate to slip a knife between his rival's ribs; or that in Shanghai a man could actually be shanghaied. I do not doubt these contingencies.

But in most of these places violence comes as an event ad hoc, from outside the normalities of life. Too often they are the material for novels or newspaper headlines. They invade and impassion the minds of men. What makes Africa's violence so unique is the uncanny sense that it is essentially *of* Africa. In a way that is not necessarily unsympathetic, it is true to say that violence is the core and fibre of Africa's being, and this those true Africans, the Negroes, Bantu and Afrikaner, fully understand.

Pure unmitigated violence, however, unrelieved by contrasts of pity and tragic sense, by depth and attenuation, by dementia or malevolence, becomes sheerest horror, or a kind of bore. In a word, brutality. It may make for a fairly accomplished sort of hell, but it does not express the arresting high drama of life, despite the excesses of adventure writers and narrators of jungle life stories. It is just here that that drop of human compassion, in the teeming, creeping, eruptive, swelling, brooding, menacing, bursting, weeping, cajoling, zigzagging charivari of life, makes

131

the spectacle become stirringly interesting.

Of course, by violence here is understood its whole protean totality, of rape and robbery; of murder and massacre; of ribald jokes and bawdy ditties; of gaudy dress and extravagant swagger; of inspired oaths and ferocious religiosity; of high falutin political declamations and many limbed terminological crocodiles.

This Shakespeare would have understood without the interpolations of the scholars, and in this wise the world of Shakespeare reaches out a fraternal hand to the throbbing heart of Africa.

Thus it comes with little surprise that the starting point in the Shakespearean odyssey for many an African who has staggered through literacy is *Julius Caesar*. There is a translation into Tswana by Sol Plaatje which loses nothing of that play's dynamism by giving it the kgotla atmosphere. But recently a friend of mine who wanted to make it more contemporary told me the tale thus.

Apparently, Chief Kaiser Msi had trampled down the haughty heads of most of the lesser chiefs in the Transkei and left them licking their bruised ambitions in the bunga to the leadership. He was so widely acclaimed by the rabble and the world at large that many of these disgruntled chieftains murmured:

> Why, man, he doth bestride the narrow world
> Like a Colossus; and we petty men
> Walk under his huge legs, and peep about
> To find dishonourable graves.

But there were other Xhosas, mostly from the cities, who resented the rapid rise of this upstart. They sought to clip his pinions, but the snag was that, being city men, it would have been hard for them to convince the tribesmen that it was in the holiest interest of the Transkei that Msi should be assassinated. A bright idea hit them! What they needed was a high-placed

Xhosa, one everybody respected, one known to be honourable, to lead the conspiracy. And who else, they thought, but that dashing, young, gallant chief, Dilizintaba Sakwe. It was tricky; this Sakwe was of the blood and the soul of honour; he would never even consider political expediency; murder would appal him; conspiracy he thought base; unless ... unless ... it touched upon the impeccable glory of the Transkei. Yes, let's get him through his love of the Transkei and his martyr-like belief in her eternal honour.

As the Americans would say, they sold him the line of how Kaiser was ambitious, and his ambition threatened the weal of the Transkei, and how Kaiser had to die that Transkei might live. These trenchant sentiments fired the heart of Sakwe, and they decided to kill Kaiser on Ntsikana's Day.

On the night before Ntsikana's Day Kaiser's wife, Nombulelo, dreamed of savage happenings. Worse still, the witch doctor, Makana the left-handed, warned Kaiser: 'Beware the Day of Ntsikana!' But Kaiser brushed these ominous prognostications aside and went to the Ntsikana celebrations.

The conspirators approached him as if they were his friends. They pleaded with him 'for the repealing of my banish'd brother' who had been sent from a Transvaal prison to Robben Eiland. Each of the conspirators pleaded for this repeal in mock obsequious manner, but Kaiser haughtily declared that he was as constant as the Southern Cross.

Then they stabbed him, one after another, and when he saw Sakwe also as one of his killers, he cried out in anguish: 'Tixo, nawe, mntwanenkosi!'

But matters were not going to be left there. A judge of the Supreme Court, investigating these dire deeds, made an interim report so alarming that the conspirators were hounded. In Basutoland to which most of them fled they were hunted by people of their own people until one by one they committed suicide in the Maluti Hills.

One thing that still reverberates in the Transkei is the magnificent speech said to have been made by a young Xhosa lawyer on the occasion of Kaiser's funeral. It is believed this speech, more than even the judge's report, inflamed the mercurial tribesmen against Sakwe and his fellow conspirators. His eloquence so roused the mob that factions forgot their feuds and went berserk in their passion to avenge Kaiser Msi.

Ah me ... that is fantasy ...

But it is more than odd how many Shakespearean situations find echo in African life.

Consider a few ...

In the Johannesburg of the 1950s there was the King of Jive, huge but electric Dumizulu. In the London of the 1580s there was jolly old Falstaff, the merriest ruffian in literature. This is no idle parallel, for just a London like that and a Johannesburg like this could produce a Falstaff and a Dumizulu.

When Sophiatown was still 'live theatre', Dumizulu dominated the shows at the Odin Cinema in Good Street. The highlight of Talent Night which fell every Tuesday was the jive contest between Dumizulu and another legendary character called Mpshe. They were a kind of Laurel and Hardy. With all his blubber, Dumizulu had a trick of making the eiderdowns of flesh around him wiggle while the pith of him stood stock-still. Indeed, all his movements spoke the infinite cheek and ludicrous incongruence of township life, and 'Falstaff sweats to death, And lards the lean earth as he walks along'.

For a fact, the relationship of Prince Hal with the ragamuffins Falstaff and Co. has reproduced itself countless times in urban South Africa. The rich man's son joining the excesses of ne'er-do-wells and, when their nefarious exploits have not come off so well, he pays for their entertainment in brothel and shebeen. Or the priest's black sheep son who gallivants with the denizens of the nether world. Have not we, most of us, looked on them with ill-concealed joy, and muttered: 'Ai, but Rev Nkabinde's son is quite a boy!' Such side-views of the human scene gave us, when the mood struck, 'argument for a week, laughter for a month and good jest for ever'.

This striking two-world contrast in South Africa has already been remarked upon by a few of our more perceptive White writers. Of course, it is the staple of the Non-White writers from *Drum*, *Zonk*, *Post*, *Elethu Mirror* and suchlike publications. But it took Shakespeare, about three hundred years ago, to report on the frolics of a high-born youth from wealthy Parktown among dubious companions in Alexandra Township. No one has told us all that Johnny has been doing in Sophiatown, Kent in Alexandra or Mike in Orlando. These boys were accepted among tsotsis, cherries and churchgoers as readily as was Father Huddleston. I wish more of the township bright boys had heard of Harry Bolingbroke.

And is it really an accident, or just another of my exaggerations, that both young Boeta Shakes and the youth of the township hanker after acting and the stage. Dramatisation, posturing, seeking special effects are so much a part of our daily lives that often we are startled when some critic says such and such an African actor was very good. All the time we thought he was just living and we were waiting for him to begin to 'act'. Perhaps this is why we necessarily exaggerate. 'Living the part', to us, does not mean seizing a role and making it part of our lives; it means pouring our exuberance into it, and God help that role. No wonder Shakespeare stepped off the boards and wrote the people's stuff. He had found out how, by pen and imagination, to hoist both groundlings and gentry right into the play.

Here is an authentic piece of township conversation. The scene is a Dube shebeen. Five chaps are sitting around with their drinks. There are labourers, one a schoolteacher and one a cop – but very much *off duty*. The big-bosomed shebeen queen rolls in and out, now and then, to serve her customers:

FIRST LABOURER: But what's wrong with the white man, hê? Tell me, folks. You can't satisfy the white man. Today, at work, the boss sent me out to the Post Office to buy stamps. When I returned, he wanted to know 'wherrer hell you been?' He said he'd been waiting for his tea since my grandfather's time. I tried to tell him about the stamps, but he hooted me out for his tea. Ten minutes after, he came to the sink, leaned in the doorway, with legs crossed and a funny smile on his mouth: 'When will you blacks grow up? I'd never've thought a man with your education would wash cups and make tea.' I suddenly felt blindingly mad, as if I could stab him, and suddenly, too, gave up.

SECOND LABOURER: Doesn't help, my mother's child. The white man's got us by the nose and he's got us by the arse.

SCHOOLTEACHER (*bitterly*): It's heartsore, my brother. Look at me. I'm educated, nè? I know what to teach and what not to teach, nè? But it breaks my heart to see what I teach just because the white man tells me that is good enough for black children. Why do I go on teaching? I've got to eat. This cop here, too, he's also a man, he's got to eat. You, too, when you get a chance to snatch a bag or grab a payroll ... (*Reminiscently*) ... Hê-ê-ê, but those boys ...

THE COP (*still off duty*): You speak true, my brother. The things that I have to do for these white men. Mcui! (*Smacking his lips and crossing his fingers*) God will hear us one day. When he asks me, me I'll say it's the white man. All those poor men I've led in a crocodile to jail, it's the white man. All those women I've left husbandless, childless, nyatsiless – God, it's the white man. Those heads I've broken, those ribs I've kicked in, those noses, those mouths, those eyes I've bashed ... God, I feel like crying, my brothers ...

A LABOURER: By right, it's croooel ...

SHEBEEN QUEEN: Hai, go away you. You've started to politika again. I don't want ma-politika here at my place! (*The tension breaks and they all laugh hilariously.*)

Now turn to *King Henry V*, Act IV, Scene 1, in the English camp at Agincourt, and listen to the dramatic irony in the conversation between King Henry, Michael Williams and

136

John Bates, wherein the common men, for a moment, speak their mind in the king's face (save that in these latter days consultation as direct as this is frowned upon). These men are obviously loyal subjects, but the king is needled and brings heavy artillery in argument against them, and later when he is alone again he erupts into that noble soliloquy on 'Ceremony'.

I choose no sides in this lofty debate. I only point to the mood in which the common men speak and think of their overlord. It is almost the apologetic voice of that cop in a Dube shebeen who utters Bates's words: 'If his cause be wrong, our obedience to the king wipes the crime of it out of us.'

But that famous 'act of immorality' committed by Othello and Desdemona fascinates me more than aught else. And appropriately it starts noisily … 'Brabantio! Brabantio!' hollers Shakespeare's arch plotter, 'Even now, now, very now, an old black ram Is tupping your white ewe!'

All the horror that one can conceive in the imagination of a backveld farmer who has tended his lambs, jealously; guarded his honour, savagely; and contemplated his women in this dark jungle of black, virile, uninhibited men, fearfully; leaps up when those words are hurled to afright the night. The tool most immediate that Iago knows he should use against Desdemona who has dared to love a black man is to 'incense her kinsmen' against the accursed union. This appeal to the herd mania is all the more remarkable when one considers that it does not come naturally to that supreme egotist, Iago.

It is not as if Iago is the kind of man who would be genuinely outraged by anything that merely concerns other men. For some people one can say that they are sincerely revolted by the 'unnatural behaviour' of their fellow men. Not so, Iago. 'Whip me such honest knaves,' he would say. But he knows that this thing that he is about to detonate touches the pack nigh and keenly. It is the most direct route to mob frenzy.

Odd now, we who live in the great cities of South Africa do

not feel so sweatily the herd animosity of the white man as do our brethren in the country. True, limply, unconvincingly the white men about us try to cast their arrogance around, but it is oft so sickly pathetic that it raises more a smile than a scowl. But we are louder mouthed. We have managed to uncurl the veneer of the white man where it has warped a little and, after the first start of surprise, we have met eye to eye with him, fallen off our haunches on our backs and guffawed.

But ...

Where we have proven that we are his equal – in evil as well as in genius – we have raised the fury in him. With a little education, a little fluent English, a little know-how, a little self-assertion and a little desiring of the sweets of his life and the women (where else at this stage will we find such charming, sophisticated felines?), we threaten his barest self-esteem. Moot, further, the fiction that we as savages are sexually more compelling, and you have announced Armageddon. You do not have to whistle at a white girl passing by. Only the crude ones among us play it that way. Cultivate yourself into a superior being; grapple with something in their world and succeed: become a scientist, a literatus, talk as if the highbrow things come naturally to you: a theory, a poem, grand passion; and especially, despite your ebony complexion, that you have a sensitive soul and cannot abide the crudities of your own people, even. Then trembling whitedom looks round at you with that curious mixed reaction of fear, wrath and horror. Écrase l'infâme!

It is just this that Othello went and done. Worse still, he made himself indispensable to the state. It is this, also, that the urban African is continually doing. He acquires degrees, if no more from Fort Hare, then Britain or America, and now dares to pontificate on the body politic or the cosmos.

But Africans, too, have vitriolic things to say about their fellows who go for white girls. Apart from the pious lie of those who declare that they never desire a white girl ...

A friend of mine tells me that if ever he got arrested for raping a white woman, he would tell the judge: 'Your Honour, I'm aggrieved that anyone could ever imagine that I would ever be attracted by a scrawny, colourless woman like that. Look at her, if you please, and tell me what is there in her meatlessness that would ever attract a man of my tastes. Allow me to bring before the court a full-blooded African woman, and I will show you where I am capable of rape. But this ... this ...'

Apart from the sour grapes, I say, many Africans sincerely believe that those of us who do manage a while to get white girls get only the scum, the what the boss wouldn't stand astinking in his backyard in any case.

So what kind of girl did Othello get? On Cassio's arrival at Cyprus, Montano asks whether Othello is wived. Cassio describes Desdemona thus:

> He hath achieved a maid
> That paragons description and wild fame;
> One that excels the quirks of blazoning pens,
> And in the essential vesture of creation
> Does tire the ingener.

Or, as the boys in Johannesburg would say: 'Nay, man, Boeta Can, you got yourself a Jewess that's got background and bodice; looks like the Lord took special time off to make her. Not one of those weather-beaten crows from Fordsburgville.' For the boys are particular about what kind of a white girl you found yourself.

By the way, let this quickly be said that, in the world that Shakespeare cast for Othello and his miscegenist doings, this kind of thing was not illegal. They had not yet come round to an Act of Immorality. The law, those days, was more concerned with whether charms and witchcraft were practised on a girl to turn her mind to unnatural love. That was a serious crime. But we in the townships have long passed that stage. City-bred loverboys who still use 'roots' to catch the girls get laughed out of the shebang.

One thing that beats me is that Shakespeare shows more compassionate understanding for Othello than he did for Shylock. Fully comprehending the painfully delicate situation, undaunted by the cruel circumstance fate had placed the man in, Shakespeare swells with the dignity and nobility of Othello's spirit. In Shylock's case, I could not escape the impression that Shakespeare joined the carping, hounding, hate-fearing, anti-Semitic rabble to make sport of the Jew. 'Tis strange, 'tis passing strange. Dammit, 'twas mean. And, fancy, in that other Venice there was hardly any risk that anyone would have peopled else the isle with Calibans.

But I wonder what we shall be like when that time comes, after we have turned the last folio, and the curtain has fallen upon all buffoonery and mock heroism and painted lives and pathetic half hopes of our little fretful spell upon the stage. What manner of men shall we be then ... or, for that matter, shall we be men?

The Fugitives

'Where the hell is Shorty? Shorty's always late!'

'You know he went for the booze.'

'So where's Mike? He's got the maps. He's the bright boy who knows all the plans. Now just when we've got to go he ain't here.'

'Look, Barnsey, you're getting jittery.'

'Shit. This isn't fun play, cheap dramatics. *This is it!*'

'Mama, give us another drink.'

'*It* my arsehole. Who d'you think you impress?'

'But where's Shorty?'   ·

'Look, Barnsey, the car's not even here. You shoot your bloody nerves into all of us. Can't we have our drink without your jitteriness?'

'T-t-to hell with you.'

'We're going there in any case.'

Poo-poo-poo-poo-poo!

'That's the car, you bastard, and I haven't even slugged my first drink.'

'It may be the cops. Somebody squealed. They know all about our plans. Let me out of here! Let me out of here!'

'Shut him up!'

'Quickly, somebody catch his throat!'

'His temple!'

'No, you'll kill him, you ass.'

'Ahhhh!'

'Untie his shoes, his belt, his underpants, his ... his tie.'

Poo-poo-poo-poo-pooo!

'They're here ...'

'Shut up, you fool!'

'Hank, you dive into that bedroom. Dive, you bastard,

I don't carredam what instructions are, dive! Tholo, Peter, Jamesy, you, you, carry Barnes out as if he was just ordinary drunk.'

'But it's only – '

'Shut up, and do what I tell you!'

'Shorty's delayed; I'm sure he's gone to that bitch of his and let us get caught here. Damn his women!'

'Shut up, you guys, *shut up!* What's happened to your discipline? Has it gone to pieces so early? When the cops come, play it easy. You're only shebeeners. Hear? You're only orrinary-to-God shebeeners.'

Poo-poo-poo-poo-poo!

'Take it easy. Hell, take it easy like me. Remember, the cops don't know you're not just orrinary shebeeners. Just take it easy, and don't make them think there's anything out of the way.'

Pooooooooooooooooooooo!

Knock! Knock! Knock! Knock! Knock!

'What the bloody hell is wrong with all you guys? Do you think I'll carry all this stuff in by myself? Jeewheezus, you guys look all dead scared. Come and help me with all the stuff in the boot of the car.'

'Shorty, you purulent pimple ...'

'Shorty, you alone?'

'Shorty, where you been all this blinking time?'

'Is it Shorty for sure?'

'Look, boys, I fetched the booze, didn't I? I fetched it alone, didn't I? I got and paid the taxi and showed him the roads, byways from Fordsburg to here. Least you could do is to carry the stuff out of the boot out there. As it is, the taxi is getting scared or tricky, and may shoot off with our whole damned party. Uncle, tell some of these boys to help me lug in the stuff, will you?'

'God. Shorty, you got us scared. Where the hell you been?'

'Scared? You scared, Uncle? Fancy Uncle bein' scared, after the big talk he gave us and after I went hell-'n-gone to get the stuff for the party.'

'To hell with you, Shorty.'

Poo-poo-pooo! Poo-poo-pooo!

'Look, you boys, unless we git out to fetch that stuff the taximan will eff-off with it all.'

'Okay, let's go. Let's all go out and git it.'

'Come-ahn, Barnsey. You too.'

'After you, sir.'

'To hell with your after yous.'

'Hey, mister, you gonna take your stuff and pay the fare and pay for my time too, or you ain't gonna like me.'

'All right. All right.'

'Take that cardboard box, Tholo. Take the other side, Jamesy. Take this box, Uncle. It's Scotch Whisky, the horse that never kicks. Uncle, it's a pity to have to drink this stuff with barbarians like these. Look out, Barnes, you clumsy fool, that box is loose under and the whole caboodle will come out.'

'Shit, git the stuff into the house. Or the cops will catch us here with the goods, us bein' the worse goods.'

'You're not supposed to talk politics on this trip.'

'Sssshh! Who talks of trips?'

'Who's that?'

'What's going on here?'

'Hush. Movement three with intent to kill.'

'Grab him! The jugular.'

'No, the larynx box first.'

'Chop! – the blade of your hand, you fool.'

'But he knows all the counters!'

'It-it-it's me, Mike, you murderous bastards.'

'Capital S-H-I-T, Mike. This isn't funny. You know we're on tenterhooks!'

'Oh-oh-okay, fellers, you've proved your point. Now, where's the party?'

Zooooom!

'Jeewheezus! Look at that taxi git the holy hell out of here.'

'Well, saves the three rand. Come, let's git the stuff into the house.'

'Wait a minute, Jane! Jaynee, it's okay now.'

'Nno! My God, no. He hasn't brought a dame, has he?'

'Jane here's going with us. Only to you she's Siporrah Medume.'

'No dame's going with us.'

'Superior instructions.'

'No dame's going with us.'

'Let's get out of this street into the house.'

'Come'n Jane – I mean Siporrah. They're rough but I think tonight just scared shit stiff.'

'Waal, and you're not scared, Michael?'

'Waal, this is the biggest thing we've tried. This is under the nose – but I'll tell you about it later. Only be careful, they're damned suspicious. Let's join them inside, shall we?'

'... and make sure, boys, you don't get too pissed. You're only allowed this drink to help you steel your nerves. You've got to have all your wits about you all the time. That's why we couldn't have the regular send off shindig.'

'Hear, hear – serve mine in a thimble, Uncle.'

'But why the macaroni should we have an unscheduled dame with us?'

'Mike, explain that one.'

'I told you, superior instructions.'

'Superior instructions from whose superior arse?'

'It isn't smart to make wild remarks like that.'

'Oh, I don't mind telling jumpy brother Barnes my little bit in the Why and Wherefore. It's true, I'm unscheduled. Nothing really vital on this trip is scheduled. It only happens there's a tricky little roundabout way from Mafeking to Ramatlhabama which I alone know, and my job is to get you through there in dead night that you cannot see, *see*?'

'Hey, who told you I want Zoda in my whisky?'

'No thanks, my dear, I don't drink.'

'How do you trust a dame that don't drink?'

'*Zoobeeriya Eenstrookshuns!*'

'When the hell is this car coming, anyway?'

'Take it easy, Barnsey, take it easy.'

'Don't keep telling me to take it easy. I bloody well told you the whole arrangement is a monumental balls-up. We'll be caught here before we've even left Joburg.'

'You don't even deserve to leave Joburg. You're entitled as of right to a nice comfy stone cell in Number Four for the rest of your life.'

'You keep getting at me, Hank. You think I'm scared of you. I'll break your scrawny neck for you.'

'You and who? You can bring your mother, your father, your brothers and sisters, your uncles and aunts, your cousins and chance relatives ...'

'Why, I'll ...'

'You'll get yours now!'

'Cut it out, boys, cut it out!'

'He's like that when he's drunk.'

'That's the general idea. Barnes has got to be made drunk first before we can leave here.'

'Pass that bottle, pally. I can't get decently pickled knowing that there's a dame here that doesn't drink, and all about "I've Got a Girl in Ramatlhabama" – the thing's got me so worried my intestines won't take it.'

'Well, son, mine are still idling just like.'

'Tell you what. Let's jazz up this party a little and forget about the Great Adventure.'

'Why doesn't Mr Superior Instructions tell us something of the hazards we take in going along with an obvious deadweight like Barnsey here? I don't like the mysterious ways in which these wonders perform.'

'Let's jazz up this party. Peter, give us a song, will you?'

'*Git on board, ah little chillun, git on board* ... Ah, what the hell, nobody wants to sing.'

'Look, Shorty, that's not thrrree fingers, and that's not whisky.'

'Easy, man. Gotta save something for the trip.'
'*Git on board ...*'
'I drink this to the success of Operation Rabbit.'
'Shhh, you bastard!'
'I guess we better sing.'
'How about "The Doughty Men"?'
'Ya, with Tholo's rumbling baritone leading us. Peter, you're Shaka. You, Mike, you're Dingane. Uncle's Gandhi, Moshoeshoe and Makana. Shorty's Moses. Barnsey's Jesus. Jane's Piet Retief.'
'Nnnnno! Who ever heard of a girl Piet Retief!'
'Duzzen marrer.'
'Come'n, Peter, give!'

Calling all the doughty men
                U-Shaka!
   Who sought and wrought
   And fought and thought:
Calling them out of the pen
                U-Dingane!
   The bloody lot
   That yielded not,
But fought from millions down to ten
Calling all the doughty men
   Le-Moshoeshoe! No-Makana!
And what the bloody hell of Pieter Retief
   Of Gandhi!
      Of Moses!
               Of Jesus!
UmKulunkulu! Give us more doughty men!

'But who wrote this moving song of the refugees? I've heard it told that it just fell together at places where fugitives have met for a night or so and wanted something to give them heart.'
'Shit, that's poetry, man – heroic poetry, and such things don't just fall together.'

'But how come Pieter Retief got into it?'

'That's the lofty part of it, son. Retief in his day must have had feelings like ours. That's what heroic poetry knows: the deeper state of a man, not just the transient things.'

'The only deeper states I know are in a bottle. Pass me a drink, lad.'

'But when's our bloody car coming?'

Knock! Knock! Knock!

'There you are, me lad.'

'Jeewheezus, the cops!'

'Ja, Martina selling liquor again.'

'Nay, baas, this is my birthday party. These are all my friends and relatives. As you can see they're all kaffirs drinking within the meaning of the Act.'

'Sure now, Martina. Let's just see their papers.'

'Aw, they rall right.'

'Hm. What beats me in this blasted job is that the kaffir's faces in their books and on their heads never tell you anything. You know, Gert, these kaffirs could all exchange their books with one another and I still would not know.'

'Ag, mahn, so long as they got the books. It's these cheeky ones that won't carry books that get me the hell in. Now, Martina, pour me a nice, large whisky, my goodly maid.'

'How come you boys can afford whisky, hey? My God, I can't. I suppose it's all stolen stuff that gets sold here in the townships at *back door* prices, nè? Not that I care much of a damn. My job is to catch Communists, not to spoil the fun of people who drink decently at home.'

'Ahhh! Enniwey, whod've thought I could drink whisky every day of my life? Soda from a siphon. Ice cubes. Bulb glasses. Ai, Martina, you are quite a girl. Now that the tsotsis drink in peace and there's less crime even at night, working in the townships is not so bad after all.'

'Well, we got to go. Martina, these friends and relatives of yours are nice boys. Give them a whisky each and put it on our account, ha, ha, ha!'

'Ya, baas.'

'Goodbyes, everybody, goodbyes.'

'Liquor on their account. Fancy!'

'Martina, these nice friends and relatives of yours, give them a whisky each on our account.'

'Ha! Ha! Ha!'

'Ya, baas.'

'Ha! Ha! Ha! Ha! Ha!'

'Goodbyes, everyone of you nice kaffirs, goodbyes.'

'HA! HA! HA! HA! HA!'

'Sure, boys, you're getting your whisky on the account of the Department of Justice. But it's coming out of *your* stock.'

'Jeewheezus. Aunt Martina, you're a spoilsport.'

'What I hated most was his saying we all look alike. Fancy, my looking like Barnsey here. I thought I had individuality.'

'Anyway, Martina pour that precious whisky, and one for yourself, too. It's probably the last we shall get from such an august source, in such illustrious company.'

'To the Department of Justice!'

'To freedom!'

'To nice kaffirs scared shat in the pants!'

'To hell with it, to Aunt Martina!'

'TO AUNTIE MARTINA!'

'There's the car, folks. We better get out of hostile country.'

'Goodbye, Aunt Martina.'

'Goodbye, Sis Martina.'

'Goodbye, Martinatjie!'

'Jeewheezus, the dear old shebeening girl's actually crying at the loss of our custom.'

'You've got the good taste of a polecat. Get into your Boy Scout uniforms, all of you!'

'What's Jane? A Girl Scout or a Boy Guide?'

'To hell with you!'

The Dube Train

The morning was too cold for a summer morning, at least, to me, a child of the sun. But then on all Monday mornings I feel rotten and shivering, with a clogged feeling in the chest and a nauseous churning in the stomach. It debilitates my interest in the whole world around me.

The Dube Station with the prospect of congested trains, filled with sour-smelling humanity, did not improve my impression of a hostile life directing its malevolence plumb at me. All sorts of disgruntledties darted through my brain: the lateness of the trains, the shoving savagery of the crowds, the grey aspect around me; even the announcer over the loudspeaker gave confused directions. I suppose it had something to do with the peculiar chemistry of the body on Monday morning. But for me all was wrong with the world.

Yet by one of those flukes that occur in all routines, the train I caught was not full when it came. I usually try to avoid seats next to the door, but sometimes it cannot be helped. So it was that Monday morning when I hopped into the Third Class carriage. As the train moved off, I leaned out of the paneless window and looked lack-lustrely at the leaden platform churning away beneath me like a fast conveyance belt.

Two or three yards away a door had been broken and repaired with masonite so that it would be an opening door no more. Moreover, just there a seat was missing, and there was a kind of hall.

I was sitting across a hulk of a man. His hugeness was obtrusive to the sight when you saw him and to the mind when you looked away. His head tilted to one side in a half drowsy position, with flaring nostrils and trembling lips. He looked like a kind of genie, pretending to sleep but watching your every nefarious intention. His chin was stubbled with crisp, little black barbs. The neck was thick and corded and the enormous chest was a live barrel that heaved forth and back. The overall he wore was open almost down to the navel and he seemed to have nothing else underneath. I stared, fascinated, at his large breasts with their winking, dark nipples.

With the rocking of the train as it rolled towards Phefeni Station, he swayed slightly this way and that, and now and then he lazily chanted a township ditty. The titillating bawdiness of the words excited no humour or lechery or significance. The words were words, the tune was just a tune.

Above and around him the other passengers, looking Monday bleared, had no enthusiasm about them. They were just like the lights of the carriage – dull, dreary, undramatic. Almost as if they, too, felt that they should not be alit during the day.

Phefeni Station rushed at us with human faces blurring past. When the train stopped, in stepped a girl. She must have been a mere child. Not just petite, but juvenile in structure. Yet her manner was all adult, as if she knew all about 'this sorry scheme of things entire' and with a scornful toss relegated it. She had the premature features of the township girls, pert, arrogant, live. There was that about her that petrifies grown-ups who think of asking for her seat. She sat next to me.

The train slid into Phomolong. Against the red-brick waiting room, I saw a tsotsi lounging, for all the world not a damn interested in taking the train. But I knew the type, so I watched him in grim anticipation. When the train started sailing out of the platform, he turned round nonchalantly and tripled along backwards towards an open door. It amazes me no end how these boys know exactly where the edge of the platform comes when they run like that backwards. But just at the drop he caught the ledge of the train and heaved himself in gracefully.

He swaggered towards us and stood between our seats with his back to the outside, his arms gripping the frame of the paneless window. He noticed the girl and started teasing her. All township love-making is rough.

'Hê, rubberneck!' – he clutched at her pear-like breast jutting from her sweater – 'how long did you think you'll duck me?'

She looked round in panic: at me, at the old lady opposite her, at the hulk of a man opposite me. Then she whimpered: 'Ah, Au-boetie, I don't even know you.'

The tsotsi snarled: 'You don't know me, eh? You don't know me when you're sitting with your student friends. You don't know last night, too, nê? You don't know how you ducked me?'

Some woman, reasonably out of reach, murmured: 'The children of today ...' in a drifting sort of way.

Mzimhlophe, the dirty-white station.

The tsotsi turned round and looked out of the window on to the platform. He recognised some of his friends there and hailed them.

'O Zigzagza, it's how there?'

'It's Jewish!'

'Hela, Tholo, my ma hears me, I want that ten-'n-six!'

'Go get it in hell!'

'Weh, my sister, don't lissen to that guy. Tell him Shakespeare nev'r said so!'

The gibberish exchange was all in exuberant superlatives.

The train left the platform in the echoes of its stridency. A washerwoman had just got shoved into it by ungallant males, bundle and all. People in the train made sympathetic noises, but too many passengers had seen too many tragedies to be rattled by this incident. They just remained bleared.

As the train approached New Canada, the confluence of the Orlando and the Dube train lines, I looked over the head of the girl next to me. It must have been a crazy engineer who had designed this crossing. The Orlando train comes in from the right. It crosses the Dube train overhead just before we reach New Canada. But when it reaches the station it is on the right again, for the Johannesburg train enters extreme left. It is a curious kind of game.

Moreover, it has necessitated cutting the hill and building a bridge. But just this quirk of an engineer's imagination has left a spectacularly beautiful scene. After the drab, chocolate-box houses of the township, monotonously identical for row upon row, this gash of man's imposition upon nature never fails to intrigue me.

Our caveman lover was still at the girl while people were changing from our train to the Westgate train in New Canada. The girl wanted to get off, but the tsotsi would not let her. When the train left the station, he gave her a vicious slap across the face so that her beret went flying. She flung a leg over me and rolled across my lap in her hurtling escape. The tsotsi followed, and as he passed me he reeled with the sway of the train.

To steady himself, he put a full paw in my face. It smelled sweaty-sour. Then he ploughed through the humanity of the train, after the girl. Men gave way shamelessly, but one woman would not take it. She burst into a spitfire tirade that whiplashed at the men.

'Lord, you call yourselves men, you poltroons! You let a small ruffian insult you. Fancy, he grabs at a girl in front of you – might be your daughter – this thing with the manner of a pig! If there were real men here, they'd pull his pants off and give him such a leathering he'd never sit down for a week. But no, you let him do this here; tonight you'll let him do it in your homes. And all you do is whimper: "The children of today have no respect!" Sies!'

The men winced. They said nothing, merely looked round at each other in shy embarrassment. But those barbed words had brought the little thug to a stop. He turned round, scowled at the woman and with cold calculation cursed her anatomically, twisted his lips to give the words the full measure of its horror.

It was like the son of Ham finding a word for his awful

discovery. It was like an impression that shuddered the throne of God Almighty. It was both a defilement and a defiance.

'Hela, you street urchin, that woman is your mother,' came the shrill voice of the big hulk of a man, who had all the time sat quietly opposite me, humming his lewd little township ditty. Now he moved towards where the tsotsi had stood rooted.

There was a menace in every swing of his clumsy movements and the half-mumbled tune of his song sounded like the under-breath cursing for all its calmness. The carriage froze into silence.

Suddenly the woman shrieked and men scampered on to seats. The tsotsi had drawn a sheath-knife and he faced the big man.

There is something odd that a knife in a crowd does to various·people. Most women go into pointless clamour, sometimes even hugging, round the arms, the men who fight for them. Some men make gangway, stampeding helter-skelter. But with that hulk of a man the sight of the gleaming blade in the tsotsi's hand drove him berserk. The splashing people left a sort of arena. There was an evil leer in his eye, much as if he was experiencing satanic satisfaction.

Croesus Cemetery flashed past.

Seconds before the impact, the tsotsi lifted the blade and plunged it obliquely. Like an instinctual, predatory beast, he seemed to know exactly where the vulnerable jugular was and he aimed for it. The jerk of the train deflected his stroke, though, and the blade slit a long cleavage along the big man's open chest.

With a demoniacal scream, the big man reached out for the boy, crudely and careless now of the blade that made another gash in his arm. He caught the boy by the upper arm with the left hand and between the legs with the right; he lifted him bodily. Then he hurled him towards me. The flight went clean through the paneless window and only a long cry trailed in the wake of the crushing train.

It was so sudden that the passengers were galvanised into action, darting to the windows; the human missile was nowhere to be seen. It was not a fight proper, not a full-blown quarrel. It was just an incident in the morning Dube train.

The big man, bespattered with blood, got off at Langlaagte Station. Only after we had left the station did the stunned passengers break out into a cacophony of chattering.

Odd, that no one expressed sympathy for the boy or man. They were just greedily relishing the thrilling episode of the morning.

The Boy with the Tennis-Racket

So Nat Nakasa, reporter, died in America. And Nat was many things, but most of all he was *Drum*. What to say? Please, not an obituary. No meaningless string of nice words. Someone said: 'Ask Can' (Can Themba, sage of Sophiatown, boisterous, beloved boozer, Professor of the Lost, now lurking somewhere in the Swazi hills). We asked Can. 'Fate,' he announced, 'is a bastard.'

Then he said this:

Someone had passed the buck to me. The story went out that a razor-sharp journalist from Durban was coming to Johannesburg to work in our main office. The editor had told someone to find accommodation for him and that someone had decided his initiation was best in my hands. Those days handing an other-town boy into my hands for initiation was subtlest excruciation. Not that we would persecute him. We only sought to divest him of the naiveties and extraneous moralities with which we knew he would be encumbered.

He came, I remember, in the morning with a suitcase and a tennis-racket. Ye gods, a tennis-racket! We stared at him. The chaps on *Drum* at that time had fancied themselves to be poised on a dramatic, implacable kind of life. Journalism was still new to most of us and we saw it in the light of the heroics of Henry Nxumalo, decidedly not in the light of tennis, which we classed with draughts.

He had a puckish, a boyish face and a name something like Nathaniel Nakasa. We soon made it Nat. I took him to Sophiatown. I showed him the room where he would stay – what was it, three minutes, five minutes? Then I took him to my shebeen in Edith Street.

There was a beautiful girl there and I hoped that Nat would make her. As a matter of cold fact, as he declined drink after drink, I decided that he was interested. She was Tswana and he was Zulu, but they got on swimmingly, love being polyglot. Honest, I don't know how it happened, but I left him there. He told me later that a few tsotsis came in and he approached them with trepidated terror. He asked them if they knew where Can Themba lived. They immediately looked hostile. (At first they thought he contemplated some harm to the revered Can Themba.) But when Mpho, the girl, explained that this was really a friend of the chap who had deserted him there on one of his drunken impulses, they said, 'Okay, Durban boy, hang around and we'll take you there.'

This is a measure of Nat's character. He was in a new situation. He knew about Joburg tsotsis, the country's worst. He was scared – he told me later he was. But he went with them, chatted with them, wanted to know what type of character his host was. Though he got only grunts, it was the journalist in action, not the terrified fish out of water.

He found me at home, out of this world's concerns. Later he found out about Joburg without the aid of my derelictions. He quickly learned about the united nations of Fordsburg and Malay Camp, about the liberal enclaves of Hillbrow, about the cosmopolitanism of Johannesburg. And about the genuine values, in those people who were not trying to prove or protest anything: God knows, South Africa begs any stranger to want to prove or protest something, and Johannesburg is its mecca.

But Nat sought for something inside himself that would make language with the confused environment in which he found himself. He sought, fought, struggled, argued, posed – but I doubt if he found it. The South African stubbornacy was too much for him and he had to go into exile.

The bitterest commentary on the South African is typified by Nat. All those Africans who wanted to be loyal, hard-working, intelligent citizens of the country are crowded out. They don't want to bleach themselves, but they want to participate and contribute to the wonder that that country can become. They don't want to be fossilised into tribal inventions that are no more real to them than they would be to their forefathers.

Nat's was such a voice. Sobukwe's is that of protest and resistance. Casey Motsisi's that of derisive laughter. Bloke Modisane's that of implacable hatred. Ezekiel Mphahlele's that of intellectual contempt. Nimrod Mkele's that of patient explanation to be patient. Mine, that of self-corrosive cynicism. But Nat told us: 'There must be humans on the other side of the fence; it's only we haven't learned how to talk.'

We replied: 'Humans? Not enough.'

One day we met at a dry cleaners called The Classic. Nat bought the drinks and said he had an idea. Ideas were sprouting all over the place, but any excuse for a drink was good enough.

After the ninth we got round to discussing the idea. Nat proposed starting a really good, artistic magazine. He wanted all of us – I don't mean just those Non-White journalists present – but all of us: Black, White, Coloured, Indian. For want of superior inspiration we decided to call the damned thing *The Classic* – the place where it was conceived, born and most of the time bred. Most of us got stinkingly drunk, but Nat captained the boat with a level head and saw to it that we met deadline.

He slipped into the artistic-intellectual set of Hillbrow and I had to go to Hillbrow. In between he met a girl who seemed to match the accomplishments he sought. She was African (that would vindicate him from the slur that any White woman was better than every Black woman, though I think Nat would have thought with contempt of this); she was educated and intelligent (though I think Nat was no snob); she was lively and interesting (though I think Nat would have none of a floosie); she would mix with the High, the Middle and the Low (Nat chose what he wanted from High, Middle and Low). Eventually, she eclipsed herself and went to marry someone in Europe.

Nat has a brother here in Swaziland, Joe Nakasa. One day Joe took me to Chesterville in Durban to meet his family. There is a father, a sister and a brother. Another brother is in England, studying at Cambridge. Their mother is in Sterkfontein Mental Hospital, unable to recognise even her sons. Nat talked little about his mother, but once when I had gone there with him, he broke out into bitter, scalding tears. I had not been there when he saw his mother, but I guessed that it was a gruelling, cruel experience.

Then he went to America. We thought this was the big break.

At the time of his death Nat was planning interesting things, journalistically speaking, interesting things ...

Quo vadis.

Cayenne Pepper

I was unconscious. I mean so high on a bit that I could have floated on air. When I came round, I had lost half my journey which I recovered at some lost and found hick-town halfway in Swaziland.

When I did get it back, it had changed. So dazingly lousy it was. I discovered that I had travelled it in cold and dust. By the time I had reached small but lovely Mbabane and safely lodged myself in it, I had dust in my ears, dust in my pockets, sockets, nostrils.

·Dust, dust, dust. Brother, dust on my lens!

But, for heaven's sake, don't rechristen this column CAYENNE DUST ON CAN'S LENS!

I will have a thorough bath before I spiral my way to school – or can somebody organise me a shot? But wait, brother, just you wait. It is first thing first everywhere on this God's globe.

Through Can's Lens

My friend Mr X C Dhlamini of Manzini is a very uncomfortable man. Usually, before he goes to his place of work in the town, he arranges with a local woman to prepare his evening meal for him, so that when he comes back late the food is ready.

Last week the woman told him that she would be going away for a few weeks into the country to visit her relatives, and for a while the meal she was preparing for him would be his last. It consisted of samp, vegetables and some succulent meat.

'I cannot remember when last I ate such tender meat,' remarked Mr Dhlamini.

After the meal, he filled his pipe and started looking for his favourite cat, called Mafufunyane, to give it its supper. The cat could nowhere be found. He looked under the stove, on the couch, in the bedroom, but there was no cat.

Back in the kitchen he eyed the remains of his meal suspiciously. There suddenly came a sick feeling in his stomach and he dashed to spill the delicious supper in the backyard. He went to rinse his mouth, and suddenly felt his cat, Mafufunyane, rubbing against his leg and purring in a friendly way.

He complained bitterly to me: 'I feel now as if I have a very dirty mind!'

The Last Shebeen

Naturally in this man's country where liquor is legal (same as you), one wouldn't expect to find a shebeen. But I found one. Trust Can Themba to find a shebeen in the Kalahari if there's one. It is in Umsunduza Township, half a mile outside Mbabane. It's probably the only shebeen in the whole of Swaziland.

Of course it's only a piccanin three-quarter affair, but already I'm on tick there for those Sundays when the Law says we can't carry liquor out.

Let the Law just say nix, and we'll be foraging ...